Ian M. Evans was born in England and grew up in South Africa. He returned to London as a doctoral student in psychology at the Institute of Psychiatry (King's College). He has been a professor of clinical psychology at universities in Hawaii, New York State, and New Zealand.

His first novel, *Forgive Me My Trespasses* (Archway, 2015) was set in a fictional public university in upstate New York. In his second novel, *The Eye of Kuruman* (Vanguard Press, 2017), the heroine travels to Botswana and rural South Africa as a public health specialist.

In *Menace*, Ian's third novel, he again draws on the setting of a campus in upstate New York—a milieu where he and his family once lived in an austere Victorian farmhouse on a hundred acres of disused dairy land, complete with classic red barn and sweeping views over Chenango Valley.

On retirement from their academic positions in New Zealand, he and his wife returned to their familiar haunts and the balmier days of Honolulu, Oahu, a place where the family love to gather.

Ian M. Evans

MENACE

AUSTIN MACAULEY PUBLISHERS[tm]

London • Cambridge • New York • Sharjah

Ordering Information:
Quantity sales: special discounts are available on quantity purchases by corporations, associations, and others. For details, contact the publisher at the address below.

Ian M. Evans
Menace

ISBN 9781947353039 (Paperback)
ISBN 9781947353046 (Hardback)
ISBN 9781947353053 (E-Book)

The main category of the book — Thriller / Suspense

www.austinmacauley.com/us

First Published (2017)
Austin Macauley Publishers ™ LLC
40 Wall Street, 28th Floor
New York, NY 10005
USA

mail-usa@austinmacauley.com
+1 (646) 5125767

Chapter 1: Menace

Curtis sat at the back of the sparse VFW hall feeling both bored and angry. He was bored because the invited speaker, a gray-haired minister from the World Church of the Creator, had been yakking on for the past forty minutes in nothing but half-truths, platitudes, and clichés.

"America," he wheezed, leaning heavily on the podium, "the greatest country in the history of the planet, is a nation of laws. If we don't control illegal immigration, we don't have a country. White folks and Christians are constantly under attack in our own country. The Muslims claim to be peaceful, but the crime rate in those communities is eight times higher than in white communities. It's not surprising that mosques here in upstate New York have been singled out. We don't know what sort of anti-American propaganda they preach in those places."

A middle-aged man near the front clapped loudly each time one of these applause lines was uttered. He was wearing a bright red T-shirt that had a design on the front resembling the well-known logo of Heinz ketchup, but which read instead:

Catch-up
with
JESUS
Blessed from
ma head to-ma-toes

What a bunch of clowns, Curtis thought. He figured the design was intended to be ironic or at least mocking of religion, but the wearer seemed comfortable with feeling blessed. Certainly, the reverend paid no attention to it and was getting into full swing:

"I've left some copies of our newsletter, *The Struggle,* on the table by the door. Help yourselves when you leave. Read how we must protect ourselves from foreigners and immigrants. Washington doesn't care about us; they even try to make people feel guilty about being white and Christian. Don't white lives matter? But now, your God-fearing neighbors are finally standing our ground and getting angry."

Curtis felt his own anger; he wanted to break something, preferably the speaker's nose for being so tedious. Maybe the windows of a mosque, that would start something, but there wasn't a mosque in Fenton. Instead, he raised his hand.

"Yes, hello, we have a question—the young man at the back in the grey sweatshirt."

"Is it *ever* a crime if a white, Christian man abuses an Arab woman?" Curtis asked. "You're saying that man shouldn't be punished, right?"

"Well, what an interesting question. I don't think I've ever been asked that before. Obviously, it depends on the circumstances, and without knowing them, I can't give you a definitive answer. But I should point out that sometimes Muslim women might be asking for it. And it also depends on what you mean by abuse—it's possible that the woman wouldn't understand our American ways and maybe judge something perfectly reasonable as abuse. Like criticizing her for wearing the hiji-thingamy. I'm not blaming them, it's just a cultural thing. They don't share our values. In my experience, Muslim women are untrustworthy…"

"But," the young man interrupted, "what if the abuse was serious—repeated physical harm and assault?"

"Well, maybe you are thinking of a domestic incident? Each situation is different there. Don't get me wrong—I'm not supporting violence," the Minister said with an innocent shrug. "We need to protect and defend our womenfolk. But again, you'd have to ask whether the woman was provoking the guy in some way, or maybe she had been sleeping around. The Bible is clear about the need for women to know their place and for those who commit fornication to be punished. Leviticus. And Saint Paul said in his Epistle to the Ephesians that wives must submit to their husbands in everything—"

A stocky, bearded man who seemed to be chairing the meeting and who didn't especially like any discussion he wasn't directing, butted in:

"Thank you, Reverend, you make real good points, and we appreciate your coming down from Albany to tell us about these issues and the need to be ultra-watchful as Muslims start to move into this community. But there are some other items on the agenda for tonight, especially Gary here, who has asked for our support to get behind the local police who have become intimidated by negative publicity across the country…well, I'll let Gary speak for himself."

Another heavy-set individual rose to his feet. He had been chatting quietly to two men seated next to him, dressed in jeans and plaid shirts. They seemed to be friends. They both applauded when Gary (one presumed) went up to the microphone, which he tapped a few times, ignoring the obvious: it had been working just fine for the past forty-five minutes.

"Look, I think everyone here knows that there is a PC element, especially in the media, that's making it harder and harder for police officers to do their job. Every scumbag and lowlife has got friends with freakin'—excuse me—video cameras. I'm not in the Fenton police department, but let's just say I'm involved with law-enforcement, and me and my fellow officers are concerned that we don't have adequate firearms to carry out our duties. We can't do our job without feeling we'll get labelled with brutality or some other crap. If we're not properly armed, both we and the troublemakers are in much greater danger because they feel cocky and willing to try something on. Believe me, we're only looking for a little citizen respect and support in this community, which has become increasingly gutless as the university has expanded here in Fenton. And about what the reverend was saying, the university has opened a special prayer room for Islamic students. Doesn't that say it all about priorities?"

"Sure Gary, I reckon all of us here know exactly what you are talking about. Being a police officer is a dangerous job, and we don't want to make it worse by bad policies or practices that give the Arabs ideas, so tell us what sort of support you had in mind. We're right behind you Gary."

At that moment, Curtis was unable to stifle a loud yawn. Everyone turned and stared at him. Gary looked up, scowling, and grabbing the microphone out of Mike's hand, shouted:

"If that little prick is a student, you should get him out of here. Maybe he's a reporter or an informer. Get him out. What's he doing here? Who invited him?"

Curtis stood up.

"I invited myself, you dipshit; this is a free country, at least that's what all you losers keep preaching…"

Seeing two guys from the audience get on their feet and move threateningly towards him, Curtis decided it was time to get the hell out. He scampered to the exit, and the two menacing goons quickened their pace. But he was nimble and was first out of the door, which he slammed in their faces, just in time to hear Mike and Gary on the dais shouting: "Go home to mommy. Don't come back here, asshole."

Safely outside, and seeing he was not being followed, the young man, recovering his dignity, sauntered to the main street in front of the fire station, climbed into his car, and drove to Chuck's Last Chance Saloon, a tough bar on the poorer end of Fenton. He ordered a local brew, 2XIPA, which made the barman sneer. *Rich college jerk,* he thought, *what's wrong with Coors?*

Curtis sat down with his beer and thought hard about the evening. Why had he even gone to the stupid meeting of STAND? This was his third meeting and these old white guys were full of shit. He'd shown up the first time after seeing a small ad on the public notice board just at the exit of Wegmans supermarket. It had read something like *Concerned about ISIS in Fenton? Concerned about the Muslim problem? Don't think it can't happen here!* Then it gave the time and place of the meeting. He just knew he had to go.

But the first night, the designated speaker from Albany canceled, and instead, he had to listen to some drivel about the sanctity of life and the evils of Jewish abortionists from a shithead from Harpursville. The same thing happened the second meeting, and the promised reverend from Albany was replaced by a general rant about how white working men and women in the region weren't winning anymore. Curtis agreed, knowing how hard his mom had to slave away at the disgusting bowling alley across the river.

Finally, on this evening, the promised talk on the threat of Islam had happened, but the level of the discussion was so goddamned banal, he could barely contain himself. Didn't matter whether these idiots had a message or not; they were so dumb they might as well let ISIS come and cut their fuckin' heads off. Then he had stupidly yawned when the other fatso started talking about guns, which interested him and made some sense at long last. *I wonder what they have against college students. Probably some sort of inferiority complex,* he reflected, trying to remember some bullshit from the introductory course in psychology he'd taken last year. He ordered another 2XIPA, and the barman finally asked him for ID, just to harass him.

Thinking of age as he put away his driver license, he realized he must have been the youngest person in the VWF hall by at least twenty years. The small crowd in attendance was not young thugs with heavy tattoos or crazy dudes in white hoods. One guy did have a plaited beard like he was a Dothraki warrior, but the nicotine stains on his fingers spoiled the illusion. The whole thing was more like a meeting of the local Elks Lodge. He'd recognized one fellow who helped out at Agway, where he sometimes stopped to pick up bags of salt in the winter for his mom. She had to keep the sidewalk to the bowling alley clear of snow and ice. Another person at the meeting he knew was the cashier at the Jiffy Lube on Riverbank Parkway—what the shit did *he* have to be angry about?

He didn't recognize anyone else, but he was sure that if he had stopped to chat to them, they would have seemed like normal, friendly, overweight, salt-of-the-earth Americans who flew Old Glory from flagstaffs in the front lawns of their double-wides and occasionally attended the Calvary Baptist Church in Fenton. They were, he knew, his own sort of people, the families he had grown up around, who decorated their modest porches with pumpkins and cornstalks in the fall. Families whose kids had gone to high school with him and who had been, like him, treated with some disdain by the self-appointed cool crowd—that small group who were the children of the academics, lawyers, doctors, and downtown Fenton business owners, who drove Priuses and Volvos.

Fenton had a quaint village atmosphere on the campus side of the river. It seemed to the casual observer such a quiet, sane little town—a college community with lots of foreign grad students and kids from downstate and aging professors. And indeed, it was. There was a trendy, fair-trade coffee bar that sold gluten-free bagels and nine different flavors of cream cheese. On Saturday mornings, there were stalls selling kale smoothies and wheatgrass juice. Okay, the little bookstore on the corner of Canal Street and State had finally closed last year, but there was still a left-leaning daily newspaper and a public library that always had a volunteer lady with long gray hair playing the harp at Christmas time.

But surrounding them were underground magma pools of barely suppressed rage and resentment stirring within the working stiffs who had dropped out of high school, and the unemployed men who had been laid off over the years and not found alternative employment, and their wives who had dreamed of something better than the bowling league and bus trips to Atlantic City. True, they were not members of the Cossacks Club, riding around on Harleys—the most dangerous thing these guys had ever driven was probably a 16-horsepower Yamaha snow blower. These were not revolutionaries or Christian soldiers. They weren't even wolves in sheep's clothing, encircling the privileged intellectual community and the snotty students of Fenton. No, they were sheep in tired, old second-hand racist wolves' clothing, pretending to be tough guys upholding the Constitution, which none of them had ever read or understood, except for the Second Amendment. They were whiners and complainers who believed every conspiracy theory they heard on Fox or read in the *National Enquirer*. Feeling hard done by, however, could make them dangerous to some—to gays, Asian computer science majors, people supporting Obamacare, and holiday home owners from downstate. But they were no threat to ISIS infiltrators.

If these bozos represented the local counter-terrorism watch, we're in serious trouble, Curtis thought. He felt again the same diffuse, undirected anger—he wanted action. He wanted to make a statement. He wanted to hit the stupid, bearded barman, who kept eyeing him in a hostile way. His mother had suggested he get some counseling. Maybe that wasn't such a dumb idea as he'd first thought. The university offered free sessions with a shrink at the student medical center. And anyway, he needed a new prescription for his meds. Planning jogged his memory. He remembered where he'd seen that Gary jerk before.

Chapter 2: Drain Brain

Professor Roger MacDonald was worried, not about the economy, or failed political promises, or radicalized immigrants, but about an unsettling disruption to his usual routine. The one thing on his schedule that morning was a mysterious committee meeting, called at the request of Jack Michaels, the new university president. He didn't know the agenda. He was told it had something to do with campus security. It was an ad hoc committee, and Roger wasn't at all sure why he'd been selected for it. Maybe it was about earthquake risk, and someone had thought a building scientist would know all about building safety. But what the heck was building science anyway? Yes, he was a full professor in the Department of Architecture and Building Science, but his field was rather more engineering, civil engineering to be precise, hydro-engineering to be even more precise.

In graduate school, a long time ago at the University of Illinois, he had made a detailed study of the design and management of waste water systems in fast growing cities as urban sprawl began to take over once-isolated suburbs and farmland. He spent some time in Paris, reviewing their system of *bouches de lavage*, or washing outlets, in which non-potable water from the Seine is released at low-pressure from curbside outlets, blocked by old pieces of red and green carpeting to keep the flow in the gutters and flush the streets of assorted debris.

The entire ingenious arrangement is made possible by a small army of men in green, who, to the puzzlement of all tourists, turn on and off the water valves and sometimes help the flow move past any obstructions. But it is also dependent on the incredible system of underground drains and sewers built under Napoleon the Third by a brilliant engineer called Eugène Belgrand. If he bumped into anyone who said they were going to Paris, Roger always provided these fascinating details to ensure they would fully appreciate the French capital.

His big break before his appointment at Chenango Valley State University was a consultation expedition—by invitation, he always explained—to New Zealand, where there was concern about rainwater run-off in coastal towns. The rainwater didn't go into the sewer system; instead, it ran unimpeded and unprocessed into the once pristine bays and inlets of the ocean. The problem was basically one of behavior change rather than civil engineering. How could you stop thoughtless citizens from pouring old paint, turpentine, household cleaners, garden weed-killer, and a thousand other nasty things directly into the open storm-water rains? His clever and inexpensive idea had nothing to do with hydro-engineering. It was to have attractive bronze plaques of fish, dolphins, crabs, and sea-horses made and installed at the openings of city drains, manhole covers, and any other accessible spot where people might be tempted to dump liquids. The message was simple: what you pour down here will end up in our gorgeous ocean.

The project was something of a success, as best anyone could measure the reduction in toxic flow, and the idea was catchy and attracted media publicity. Suddenly, Roger MacDonald was a minor celebrity—less than a minute of fame, but enough to get a tenured appointment at CVSU, where he was occasionally written up as one of the world's foremost experts on drains. Well, it was a strange thing to be known for, but before long he had acquired the nickname, the moniker, *Drain Brain*. It was a genuinely funny twist, and although he usually scoffed and pooh-poohed when it was said to his face or mentioned in the campus newsletter, he secretly delighted at this sign of peer acceptance and student appreciation.

"Drains can be fascinating," he'd try telling classes, "you don't think much about them until they get blocked, and then you are in trouble. Big trouble." There was a whole course on drains and drainage issues in the building and construction science degree. Some of his colleagues thought that was a bit much. But of course, the students needed to know the science of drains and how to design them. Some of the students could be kept interested in practical matters, and he had a couple of amusing PowerPoint presentations on the causes of domestic drain blockage and how to clear them, and what to check on if you were buying an older house. It was kind of fun, and the students enjoyed expressing their disgust at hair, gunk, and wet wipes, but it didn't take away from the reality that he had essentially a boring specialization and was, to put it bluntly, a rather pedantic professor.

One other experience had cemented, if that was the appropriate term, his relationship both to drains and to the university. When the State of New York had selected the site for one of their new star colleges, they were attracted to the Chenango Valley region and to the pretty, state-owned lakes in an unfrequented woodland area near the old canal system and the Chenango River. Because the area was swampy and prone to flooding every spring when melting ice blocks on the river piled up and stopped its flow, the builders and architects had had to design an extensive system of large underground drains.

The idea was to ensure the campus would never flood, and it was a good one, except for one thing. To create a gorgeous landscape, a park-like atmosphere to soften the red brick and concrete architecture popular in the campus building boom of the sixties, the planners had incorporated two small lakes, Lily Lake and the larger Chenango Lake, into the landscaping of the campus. It was a fabulous idea and allowed for pleasant walkways, short hiking trails, and even some canoeing and row-boating on the larger lake. But there was a fatal drawback, which was that in the event of a once-in-a-hundred-years rainfall in south-central New York, the lakes themselves would overflow and flood water would back up into the campus.

It was totally unlikely, said the engineers at the time, but of course a once-in-a hundred-event could happen twice in fifty years and then not again for two hundred. In the late nineties, the statistically improbable flood happened twice in consecutive years. The library basements were flooded, as were some of the zoology labs and the art museum's archival room; plant science lost rare hybrids they'd been developing, and the president's rather grand mansion was badly damaged. It was Roger MacDonald's second life-changing professional moment. He was asked to study and review the entire system of tunnels and drains, develop computer models, and suggest new patterns of water flow that could be constructed. He spent a lot of time crawling around underground and got his photo in the Fenton Times wearing a hard-hat and a geeky smile. His only two graduate students posted the article on the bulletin board outside his office.

Roger urged them to take it down, but he was secretly delighted by the notoriety. Drain Brain had become a campus institution. All he had to do now was coast along for the next eight or nine quiet years, watching his TIAA-CREF retirement fund grow. At sixty-six, he could maximize his Social Security benefits and retire in comfort—he wasn't sure where, given that both sons and their families were in cold places. Maybe Florida somewhere, where the grandkids might like to visit. He was comfortable and reasonably secure, financially as well as emotionally. When the weather allowed it, he did a little gardening.

Roger looked in the mirror after a quick work over with his electric razor and thought, without rancor, what an ordinary sort of fellow he was. He patted his tummy disconsolately. He'd been gaining weight; 'middle-aged' spread he liked to call it. But call it what you want, he needed to go to the gym more often. It was difficult to be motivated, living alone. His two boys, now adults, were off on their own, one in Boston and one in Rochester, New York. They were both high school science teachers. After his wife had died unexpectedly of an aggressive form of ovarian cancer just a few years ago, Roger had been disinclined to date. In any case, Fenton was a small town and the opportunities were limited. He had friends, mostly colleagues at the university, and he went out to dinner occasionally with buddies. But he hated to go to the movies on his own, so he watched a lot of Netflix on his large screen TV. He liked driving down to the city where he stayed overnight at the Empire Hotel—CVSU faculty got a ten percent discount.

The anonymity of New York suited him—he could go to plays and concerts alone, like thousands of others, and not feel embarrassed. He missed his wife, but he loved his cat.

Ordinary or not, and routine as his lifestyle had become, he was pretty content, he thought, as he finished tying his tie. There's nothing like the quiet life. Grabbing his shoulder bag that held his laptop, he let the cat, Eugène, out the front door, clambered into his 2004 Volvo S80, and headed off to campus.

Chapter 3: The Meeting

Roger MacDonald made his way to the University Council's boardroom in the administrative building, which was named after a former governor of New York State. The rather luxurious venue shouldn't have surprised him, but it always took him slightly aback—he had only been in it occasionally during his entire tenure at CVSU, and he'd forgotten the paneled walls, the huge conference table, and the oil paintings of dead white males. Governors? SUNY system presidents? He didn't recognize any of them. He looked around for an empty chair and spotted one next to Dave Gordon, whom he knew reasonably well.

"Hey, DB, howzit?" asked Dave cheerfully. "What are you doing here?"

"I might ask you the same question, Dave," Roger said, as he lowered himself into the leather swivel chair. "I know you're retired because I came to your farewell roast. Why are they dragging you out of mothballs? What do you know about earthquake safety?"

"Earthquake safety? Shit, maybe I'm at the wrong meeting. I was invited to a hush-hush do about campus security."

"Yeah, well, me too—I just assumed—given my background—it was about building safety."

"No, I don't think so. I figured it was more about terrorism and violence on campus and being prepared and all that. I've been dabbling in the problems of sexual assault on campus and I assumed that's why I was invited. Who's running this show anyway? The dean of Social Sciences is already here, so is the provost, but I don't recognize most of the others. They seem to be waiting for someone. I didn't get an agenda."

At that moment, Jack Michaels, the president of Chenango Valley State University, strode forcefully, but with a noticeable limp, into the room and sat at the head of the table. Greta, one of his assistants, closed the doors in an ostentatious manner, like at a papal conclave of the College of Cardinals.

"Good morning all," Michaels began, "welcome and thanks for coming. I'm not sure how long this meeting will last, but I've ordered coffee to be brought up in half an hour and I'm hoping we can wrap it up by then. I want to keep this meeting confidential, which is why you did not get a detailed invitation. I asked Susan," he continued, nodding towards Susan Kraus, the provost, "to put together a few names of campus movers and shakers who might offer advice on a complex matter. As I've only been in this position a few months, I'm not sure of the previous history, and I want to make sure those of you who have been around and are wise to campus matters and campus politics get a chance to offer your sage counsel. I want to reaffirm this meeting is off the record; it's a chance to talk among ourselves. You all know Greta here, my PA—I've asked her in as a check on my memory, but she won't be keeping minutes. To circumvent State sunshine regulations, I'm not even calling it a meeting—more a discussion, an advice-giving session for the new boy in town. Can I have a show of hands that you agree with these conditions?"

Everyone's hand went up, Roger's rather slowly. Frankly he didn't like secrecy and he didn't like campus politics. Dave nudged his elbow and hissed, "Get your hand up, DB!" Dave himself loved campus intrigue and was dead keen to find out what the hell it was all about, and why they needed a professor emeritus of clinical psychology in the room. He'd rather come to accept that his moving and shaking days were over.

Michaels looked around the large conference table and continued. "Thank you, gentlemen—and ladies—for your commitment. I assume you all know each other, and I don't want to waste time on introductions, but when you start to speak, as I hope you will, please just state your name and your title at that time.

"I want to review our campus policy regarding guns on campus. I've been told that back in the late eighties, the campus security department requested my predecessor they be armed. That sounds like a reasonable request to me—apparently they had encountered some dangerous and violent situations. And they felt enfeebled when there was an armed offender on campus, and they had to call in the Fenton police for backup. But there was a strong student protest, sit-ins and marches were held, classes were disrupted, and I think most of the faculty sided with the protesters. The plan was shelved.

"But, over time, campus security has become centralized; now our campus police are part of New York State University Police, and gradually firearms were allocated without anyone noticing. There have been no serious incidents and the campus police have focused more on safety on campus at night. That sort of thing. After 9/11, however, the mood of the country changed and the campus with it, I think. As most of you know

I was on active duty during the second Iraq war. It was obvious that even back in the homeland life was becoming more dangerous, security issues were on everyone's mind, CVSU started to screen foreign students much more judiciously. Then seven years ago, we had that terrible incident down the road in Binghamton, when a Vietnamese immigrant killed thirteen people at the citizenship center downtown. He had two Beretta pistols—a forty-five and a nine millimeter, I know them well— with a New York State license for both. Since then, the pressure has been on us and our policies. You will know that across the country some faculty are demanding to bring their guns into the classroom for their own protection, if students have legal carry.

"Last week matters came to a head. I received a formal deputation from campus security asking me to issue them with semi-automatic rifles and requesting they be allowed to carry them on campus rather than be locked away in cruisers or the main office here in this building. They brought me a report from the FBI saying a shooter on campus represents a special risk to students and any responding officers, because their handguns are not the most suitable way of taking down a shooter. I figured it would be a major step, and I wanted to hear from you as a group to get some measure of what the campus reaction might be. I want to stress this is up for discussion and I remain a hundred percent open-minded. Of course, I did not invite anyone from campus security to this discussion. Right, open for debate."

There was absolute silence in the room. Roger and Dave turned and stared at each other, with expressions of total disbelief. Someone from the other side of the table blurted out:

"In the immortal words of John McEnroe, 'you cannot be serious'!"

Michaels frowned. "Oh, I'm serious, all right. But let's not have a free for all. If you have something to say, raise your hand or signal to me and wait to be recognized. I don't want to kill any discussion, and I want everyone to be heard. Robust debate is the standard in this school. Yes, Joe, your hand is politely raised."

"Hi, President Michaels and faculty, my name is Joe Stiglioni, and I'm deputy chief of city police here in Fenton, representing the chief who couldn't make this meeting. Our position in the Fenton police department is that we are opposed to this request. The officers on campus are okay, they're good guys, and we work closely with them. But they don't have the same kind of training, or experience as we do. Fenton police are only five minutes from campus and we're always on call. We're the professionals. Give those guys semi-automatic weapons, and they are more than likely to shoot each other—or innocent students."

"Thanks Joe," Michaels countered hastily, "so in your view it is largely a matter of further and more intensive training for the campus officers. But I'd like to note the campus officers making the request pointed out that as all of them like to go hunting in deer season, they're better with a rifle than with a handgun—it gives them greater range and more accuracy. And a bad shot with a rifle is better than a good shot with a handgun."

"And greater firepower and greater danger to bystanders," Joe interrupted, "but you put words in my mouth. It's not simply a matter of increasing training—it's their background, their experience, their professionalism, the scope of their mission, their sense of importance, which, you should know, we think to be seriously inflated. Look at the pressure right now against the whole militarization of police departments. We get enough flak as it is. The campus police have a designated role, and it is, or should be, community-focused. If they encounter a dangerous criminal, a mental case, or a terrorist, they need to call on us. That's what we handle."

"Every single day," he added, a little melodramatically.

"Well, we don't want to be stepping on anyone's toes, but let's not turn this into a turf battle. You on the end, you've had your hand up patiently, what do you want to say?"

A man Roger didn't recognize, but he thought might be the dean of the School of Communication and Journalism, asked hesitantly: "I don't quite know why all this secrecy is necessary, unless you know ahead of time there will be strong objections. Why not just have a full campus debate on the matter?"

Michaels was ready for this. "I'm not yet sure it is such a contentious matter, Frank. I have contacted one of the schools in Georgia where the campus police patrol openly with semi-automatic rifles. Their president told me excitedly that applications to their school have gone up eighty percent. Apparently, parents are concerned about campus shootings. As you know, we've all had terrible publicity about the frequency of rape on campuses—the latest survey suggests one in five college women experience such assaults. Parents are alarmed about safety, and college campuses have been vulnerable in the past. You'll find that if there is any student and faculty opposition it will be out of step with the mainstream."

"I'm not sure a casual phone conversation constitutes adequate data, President Michaels, and anyway let's hope we are not making policy decisions based on future enrollments."

"I think you will find, Frank, that for the future of your journalism program, enrollments *are* the most important considerations."

There was a shocked silence in the room. Michaels realized he had come on far too strong and had to back away from such a blatant show of hostility. He looked around anxiously and saw an attractive young woman with long light brunette hair falling onto her shoulders, a sort of Kate Middleton look. She was holding up her hand with her elbow still on the table. Maybe she'd be safer, although she looked half the age of everyone else.

"Yes, the young woman on the end there. I'm sorry I don't know your name—"

"Thank you, Professor Michaels. I'm Katrina Moss. I'm the clinical psychology intern at the university counseling and health center. I'm representing the counseling program director, Dr. Barbara Kennedy, and the head of the center health division, psychiatrist Dr. Abidi, who was invited but said he couldn't come. I don't think they realized this was such an important or secretive meeting, or maybe they wouldn't have sent me. But I know about confidentiality, and Dr. Gordon, sitting over there, can vouch for me, as I'm a graduate of the clinical program he directed until his retirement last year."

Dave Gordon smiled and gave a little wave and then turned to Michaels and offered a slight nod of the head in approval. He was tickled pink by her self-confidence, her eloquence, and her good sense. But he was more curious as to what she would say.

"The only point I want to make is that when it comes to students on campus who might be or become dangerous, we have introduced extensive training and protocols on the detection of violence, on response strategies, prevention, and de-escalation methods. And we worked with Campus Security, who was always helpful. It seems our focus can be on detection and prevention—ever since Seung-Hui Cho's outrage at Virginia Tech, we've been concentrating on better assessment and prediction and help for troubled students. That is our emphasis at the Center, and I have to say—although this is a personal response, and I cannot speak for Doctors Kennedy and Abidi, of course—we would be quite concerned at the idea that the campus security guys, whom we rely on if we have a patient who is out of control, would come to assist us with semi-automatic weapons in their hands."

The room broke out in muted applause, and some shouts of "Well said," and "Right on," and someone whispered, "Sanity from the mental health expert, if not from our administration."

Provost Susan Kraus looked uncomfortable, but she was loyal. "I know many of you are not in favor of guns on campus, but you lost that battle years ago. Ever since '09, the issuing of firearms on state owned campuses is at the pleasure of the campus president. President Michaels is showing you a great deal of respect by having this meeting and getting your opinions, please let's try to reciprocate and have a respectful discussion of pros and cons. We can't turn this into a referendum on gun control. I think President Michaels is looking for a policy that will satisfy the campus police, the need for security on campus, and the principles and ideals of the faculty, the students, and the local community, especially

Assistant Chief Joe Stiglioni. We do need to think about this constructively and rationally and calmly. We all want to do what is best for the campus community."

Roger turned to Dave Gordon and whispered, "Aren't you going to say something, Dave?"

"Aren't you? I'm retired, it's not my campus anymore."

"Yes, but they respect you. You're a force majeure."

Dave raised his hand. Michaels relieved there was someone else in the room whose name he knew, responded immediately, despite others having had their hands up longer. "Yes, Dave, what's the word from psychology?"

Dave stood up and adjusted his glasses. "If you go hiking in Alaska in the fall, it can be dangerous. There are lots of big bears who can be exceedingly aggressive. So there are two schools of thought. Always take a rifle with you for protection, or never take a rifle with you. My view is never to take a rifle, because a rifle makes you overly confident, not cautious, and, if a bear charges, you may be so scared and your hands would be shaking so much you don't have a hope of hitting the poor thing. If you go hiking without a rifle, however, you look where you are going, exercise caution, don't go stomping about in a wild blueberry patch, and if you see a bear, you back away slowly and carefully. That's the word from psychology."

Dave sat down to total silence and furrowed brows. A few people, maybe processing the analogy quicker than others, were grinning. Michaels looked annoyed.

"I can tell you've never been in a war zone, Dave. When you encounter bears out there you can be damn sure you'd want to have a fully loaded M16A4 assault rifle in your hands."

"But this isn't a war zone, Jack—"

29

"And we're not on a hike through the blueberry bushes, Dave."

"True. I suppose it boils down to different perceptions of threat. Miss Moss, Katrina, made the point well. We need to be vigilant. We need to look for signs. Maybe we need to train the faculty better to spot troubled students. We need to train them to recognize bear scat. We don't need to over-react, and frankly I'd predict that if the campus police started patrolling around with semi-automatic rifles, both the faculty and the students would go ballistic. You'll have massive protests because no one will feel safer, quite the opposite. Look, we know that New York State has strict gun control laws; we like that. But in the past, some of my colleagues have expressed anxiety that in the current political climate there's nothing stopping our students from bringing a concealed weapon onto campus, even into the classroom. The only way to prevent this is by having a social consensus that it would be very wrong and anti-social. Start having weapons all over campus, and the Second Amendment crazies would escalate the discussion. They'd insist on their rights, you'd be under much greater pressure, and the whole campus ethos would change. It's a terrible idea, Jack."

Again, scattered applause greeted Dave's remarks. Susan Kraus took some control. "Listen everyone, as we expected, this is a topic that raises lots of passions and different perspectives. I think President Michaels took an excellent first step by getting a sense of the campus mood and opinions, but not everyone has spoken. What I'd like to suggest is that we now form a smaller committee to discuss the matter and try to write some policy statements that the president will find helpful as he wrestles with these issues. Like it or not, state law gives him the authority to make these decisions unilaterally. He has graciously offered a chance for others to weigh in, and I'm sure he would like to establish a rational policy that is acceptable to most and which will provide maximum security for our campus. If it's okay with you Jack, I'll invite the participants here to contact me if they are willing to serve on that committee, and I'll select just four or five representative people to see if we can develop a written policy for your consideration."

Jack Michaels looked relieved.

"That's why you're the provost, Susan, excellent diplomatic skills. By all means, let us leave it there for this morning, but, as I said, I remain open. Feel free to email my PA if you have any further thoughts to consider, and be sure to volunteer for Provost Kraus's little committee group. Thanks all, we're adjourned for today, but be sure to stay and have a cup of coffee and keep talking among yourselves if you wish."

His comment about Susan's 'little committee' sounded to most like a put-down, but the provost didn't blink, she just smiled and nodded.

"Whew, Dave, that was a bit tense," Roger said as they pushed their chairs back and stood up to leave. "I didn't know you knew anything about bears. Hey, it's almost lunchtime. Do you want to join me for a bit of lunch? There are a couple of others who look like they'd want to talk. Let's debrief."

"Sure," Dave replied, "screw the coffee—it's after eleven and we can get a beer at Valley Garden."

Chapter 4: Discussion

Valley Garden was the name of one of the many cafés on campus, but it was the favorite haunt of the faculty because this one had a license to serve alcohol. Faculty often met there at the end of the day, had a beer or a glass of wine, a plate or two of nachos, and sat around on the concrete benches surrounding concrete tables, shooting the breeze about life in the university and what some idiot department chair had recently proposed. The tables had a hole in the middle and once the spring weather warmed up—usually not until the end of April in the Chenango Valley—the staff would put up bright orange umbrellas, and the faculty groups would sit outside, pretending it was warm enough to do so. On this particular day, it was a few weeks before the end of the spring semester and was surprisingly warm. Three other colleagues from the university president's meeting joined Dave and Roger at their table, and Dave had collared Katrina and asked her to lunch with them. Once they had collected their beers and two large orders of pita and hummus, they all leaned in, semi-whispering, in a conspiratorial fashion. And as the table only allowed seating for six, they could ensure, in a socially appropriate way, that no one else joined in their discussion.

"Whew, that was septic, wasn't it? I was damn sure the president had already decided it would be a great idea and he expected us all to fall into line."

Karl was one of three campus safety officers—their job was to enforce safety procedures around the campus labs, especially chemistry and other areas where there were hazardous materials. Dave knew him well because when he was Chair of Psychology, one of the psychophysiology labs was cited for not having proper exhaust fans in their fume hoods. Karl had been reasonable and worked with Dave to ensure compliance.

"My thoughts exactly," Dave responded. "I don't think we'll need safety officers any more—everyone will be shooting each other. Overloaded electrical outlets in faculty offices will be the least of your worries, Karl."

"Jeez, Dave, it's not funny," said Marcia Kastanowicz, "Michaels is a maniac. I knew it would be a disaster if we appointed a goddamned general to be president. You know I'm on the Faculty Senate? When the three candidates for Sarah DeLorean's replacement were announced as finalists by the Council, we passed a unanimous resolution that a retired general was unacceptable…"

"Well, Marcia, that just confirms the Senate has no power and no voice, which is why I resigned ages ago. But given that it became widely known who was most opposed to Jack's selection, why did he invite you to his top-secret security meeting?"

Marcia, who was a professor of organic chemistry, grinned.

"Because he knows you should keep your friends close but your enemies closer, of course. That and the fact that I've just been appointed to a national consensus panel to advise the State Department about the risks of the newer generation of chemical weapons. I got a lot of media attention for my paper on our old chemical weapon stockpiles, which I cleverly called 'Agent Orange or Aging Lemon?'"

"I thought Agent Orange was an herbicide, not a chemical weapon?" Karl asked.

"I wouldn't make the distinction—it was a weapon of war and terribly destructive. Parts of Vietnam are still highly contaminated with dioxins and there are some astronomical rates of cancers in the population. Remember when the fire in the basement of the State Office Building down in Binghamton in 1981 spread dioxins and PCBs throughout the building? We were all grateful that Fenton was well north and our valley basically upwind. These chemicals are deadly, as you know, Karl, but now we have a whole lot of new agents and, thanks to the Syrian government, jihadists have no difficulty in getting their devil hands on some of them. Arming the campus police to the teeth wouldn't be much help if we had that kind of attack."

Roger looked around the group. The discussion was disjointed, a strange blend of the knowledgeable and the superficial. It was what he often found most irritating when interacting with his faculty colleagues. They had loads of detailed information about trivial things, but their left-wing leanings often led them to exaggeration and over-generalizations. They knew the answers to every question, but they had no actual influence on anything, just like Dave had said about the Faculty Senate. He turned to the sixth person seated at the table, who was drinking a Yuengling and eating a lot of the pita bread—Phil Cohen, an associate professor in the History Department.

"What do you think Phil? You're an authority on military strategy and defense policies— what did you think of this strange meeting we had? Didn't Michaels at least ask for our opinion? He could have just gone ahead and made an executive decision; at least that's what I learned at the meeting. Much to my amazement, I might say."

Phil stroked his beard a few times, a sure sign he was thinking and that his thoughts were going to be wise ones.

"I've read some of Michaels' articles. He's got an okay scholarly record. He published parts of his Ph.D. dissertation in the *Journal of Strategic Studies*, which is a decent journal. I don't remember the details, it wasn't in my area, but it was something about the leadership style of General Omar Bradley. Oddly enough I've read that Bradley's key characteristic was never to let his ego get out of control or in the way of consultation, but I don't think our new president is following that example, judging from his performance today. I was underwhelmed by how he managed the meeting and failed to project an air of impartiality. Why ask people for input if you make it clear ahead of time that you've made up your mind? And I think he was visibly thrown when you, Katrina, were one of the first to speak up, and basically you are still a graduate student, aren't you, although what you said was about the best comment of the meeting. But why didn't your shrink show up? Surely he was invited?"

"Sure, he was. Ali just called me and asked if I could go in his place. He said he couldn't attend. He didn't say why. He sounded a bit agitated, I thought. He said he'd tried to get Barbara Kennedy, my boss and the director of the counseling program in the center, to go, but she was out of town. I asked

Ali if I needed to contact someone to say I'd be coming in his place, and he said better not to."

"Anyway, Kat, it was brave of you to speak up when it was obviously a top-secret meeting—I loved the touch of ceremoniously closing the council-chamber doors. And yeah, I think Michaels was thrown." Dave Gordon was smirking.

"Hell, Dave, I hope he doesn't try to punish me! Call me paranoid but I've been getting some phone calls at the clinic in which no one answers at the other end, and after a few moments of me saying 'hello, hello' there is the distinct beep of someone hanging up." Katrina was smiling and did not appear too concerned.

Roger listened to the conversation around the table. They were getting increasingly off topic. He stood up.

"Thanks, folks, but I've got to go. Interesting as this has been, it doesn't seem like we've discussed what we're going to do to stop the president from approving a whole raft of new weapons for the campus police. I'm worried about the students and their reaction to this. Most of our students are from downstate. Compared to the five boroughs, they think Fenton is the safest place in the world. I don't see the point of disillusioning them. And the local students from around here probably grew up from a young age hunting deer and shooting squirrels. They're pretty used to handling sporting rifles and shotguns, but I'm sure they don't want to see the campus police parading around with assault weapons. I'm going to volunteer for Susan's committee, and I hope you all do the same. We need some voices of sanity and restraint even though I didn't see much of it during this lunch. But don't we have to be reasonable, like Katrina here? If we're going to rely on the police for security, don't we have to respect their views? Bye all."

As Roger walked away to the trash bins to dump his plastic glass and paper plate, the others looked at each other. Dave reflected the consensus in their facial expressions.

"DB's being a bit prickly today, isn't he? I wonder what's eating him. Surely we're all as anti-guns as he is?"

Chapter 5: The General

Jack Michaels was only five-foot-six, but he had a barrel chest, in fact a barrel body. When he was a boy growing up in Charleston, no one messed with him; there are some real advantages to being a mesomorph. Not that he grew up in an environment where people were likely to mess with each other. His father was a mid-ranking officer in the army, and as a boy Jack had lived in military housing where there was a degree of civility and respect. If you liked hitting people, join the boxing club; if you liked scrapping, play football. He didn't like either. Jack liked reading, history mostly, playing the clarinet, and making video movies. Betamax was still popular when he was a teenager.

When his father suggested he go to college at The Citadel, he pleaded with his mother to try to change his dad's mind. He wanted to go to Vanderbilt. "We couldn't possibly afford it," his mother had said. "But I'll talk to dad, and I'm sure he'll agree that if you apply and get a significant scholarship, you can go. Otherwise apply to The Citadel—in-state tuition is manageable. And its focus is on leadership."

He was not offered a scholarship to Vanderbilt and reluctantly went to The Citadel. Grudgingly, he had to admit the courses were good; some of the professors were real scholars. He did a double major in history and psychology. Their rigor suited his temperament. He even began to enjoy the discipline. He enrolled in the army ROTC and took courses from the Department of Military Science, which cut down his tuition fees still further. He didn't play any sports, but he kept fit at the gym. After graduating, it was easy to get a commission in the Army—in fact he was offered one, at the rank of Captain. His grades were noted; they wanted him in cerebral areas assigned to the top brass—strategy, leadership development, foreign relations, security, and interrogation. His psychology background was considered relevant. He gained wide experience, worked hard, and he was regularly promoted. His father was impressed.

Nine/eleven changed everything. By April 2003, he was on active duty in Iraq, no longer sifting through policy documents and attending seminars on tactics at Fort Meade. He was needed on the front line. He was assigned to lead a top-secret task force charged not with discovering weapons of mass destruction—it was clear there were none—but with trying to work out why the rumors had developed in the first place, who started them, why Saddam thought it would be a fun game to keep implying that maybe he had them. It was all about the phony intelligence and the motives of various key players in the administration. He didn't know for certain, but he guessed the President himself wanted this sort of information. George W. Bush was going to take a lot of heat for starting such a disastrous war on false pretenses. So was the Secretary of State, Colin Powell. They needed to find out if they had been duped, deliberately misled—had some person, or persons, known what the infamous but harmless aluminum tubes were really for?

Jack was promoted to Colonel and given high security clearance. The information was sensitive, and informants were terrified. The stakes were high, and Michaels established a reputation for ruthlessness. No one knew whether it was justified, but sometimes a reputation, even if not warranted, serves you well. There was a rumor of his 'forcing' family members to spill the beans on the activities, not of combatants, but of civilian scientists who had possibly worked on chemical weapons. To find out who had been deceiving whom, he conducted skillful interviews, recognizing the cultural mores which allowed him to come across as sympathetic. And he sifted through intelligence reports, visited sites that were still suspicious, and badgered technical experts who could make sense of mysterious looking equipment and knew what yellowcake uranium was. He even got to interview Hans Blix, the chief UN weapons inspector, to find out what he truly thought about the existence of weapons of mass destruction, and his level of certainty.

Jack began to understand how suspicion altered perceptions of reality and how fear of underestimating threat levels led to judgments of probability that could be serious miscalculations. His knowledge of psychology and irrational thinking and distorted cognitions was far more relevant to these probability estimates than to strategies for forcing confessions out of religious zealots. The extreme tactics didn't work, anyway.

A year later, when he was traveling with his intelligence unit, a refreshed insurgency, who hadn't heard President Bush announce that the mission was accomplished, destroyed the jeep in front of his convoy with an IED, and he and all his comrades came under unrelenting mortar fire. They were eventually relieved by another nearby unit, but Colonel Michaels sustained a significant injury to his right ankle. After weeks in the hospital, two emergency surgeries, and ongoing rehabilitation, he was walking again, but with a limp.

He never told anyone he hated Iraq. He couldn't stand the place. The dangers were constant. The people were duplicitous, unreliable, scheming, without a shred of loyalty to any cause. The religious tensions reminded him of the worst of the Protestant-Catholic conflicts in the European wars of religion nearly four hundred years before. He came to despise Arabs and the Muslim faith, though he knew enough never to express such feelings, recognizing that having had some of his friends blown to smithereens in front of his very eyes contributed to his hatred. He had enough insight to know it was irrational, prejudicial, and potentially harmful. He had already lost control in one situation, and a covert operation had gone horribly wrong, but the army had covered for him, buried it, and cleared his name.

He requested a transfer, a posting in Hawaii. Tripler Hospital, the pink art deco masterpiece on a hillside overlooking the airport and Pearl Harbor, was able to provide the one final surgery required for his ankle. His request was accepted. Confidential fitness reports described him as still edgy, but he had a broad range of special analytic skills that could be useful anywhere. Hawaii was a good place to help him regain some composure, and he soon got his third star. It was not an arduous tour of duty, in fact quite the opposite. He had plenty of free time to work on policy issues. He applied to Pacific University to enroll in their Master's degree in Diplomacy and Military Studies. He did extremely well and was eagerly accepted into a doctoral program in military history, one of the best in the country—ironically at Vanderbilt

University. So, in 2008, at the age of forty-nine, he was released from active duty, and he moved to Nashville, Tennessee, with Tomoko Tanaka, a divorced Japanese-American woman he had met on Bellows Beach one Sunday. Being on a Marine Corps base with gentle waves, the spot was popular with military families. Tomoko, who was feeling lonely, made the first approach. Jack felt needed. Friends were astonished when they got married—some people had thought he was just too set in his ways.

When he finished his Ph.D. only two years later, he applied for an academic administrative position at one of the smaller four-year SUNY campuses in upstate New York—his mother had come from Albany and he had family ties in the region. Tomoko had hoped to return to Honolulu, but she quite liked Brockport; it was quaint, and Rochester was nearby. By 2013, he was their Vice-President for Administration and Facilities Management. It was a good position, but didn't quite fit his personal ambitions. It seemed rather a come down. If he could be a president at a large, major university, he felt he had a lot to offer—academic qualifications, now some academic management experience, but most of all a past record of distinguished, highly responsible service as a senior office in the United States Army, only slightly below Chief of Staff of the Military Intelligence Corps, motto: *Always Out Front*. He thought the phrase was a bit corny, but better than having jokes about 'military intelligence' being an oxymoron. He had considerable contempt for people who made those kinds of snide remarks. Good men, and one good woman, had been killed in front of him. He didn't have PTSD, but he could never forget the horror of that surprise attack.

Why hadn't they been better prepared or forewarned? Where was that intelligence when it was needed most? He didn't like surprises. Good thing Tomoko, about his age, didn't want children. After they were married, she gained quite a bit of weight, something he saw as a slight sign of weakness, but it didn't bother him and he never said anything to her. He exercised as much as his damaged ankle allowed. Swimming was especially good for maintaining his fitness. He could keep his life in control. He wasn't rigid so much as structured. His colleagues at the college quite liked him. He was thoroughly predictable and transparent, and his wife threw decent parties—lots of homemade sushi and fresh fruit her family flew in for them from the Big Island. But he was restless—he needed a challenge.

University councils and boards of regents around the country were becoming attracted to former military officers as top administrators. They talked at length about leadership skills, and they seemed insensitive to the fact that faculty would despise a president or chancellor who had had no university experience and no higher degree. But Jack Michaels expected a much warmer reception as he did have a Ph.D. and had publications. When an executive head-hunting firm contacted him, and told him about the position at Chenango Valley State, he was delighted. Here was a highly-regarded college, sadly not Ivy League, but right up there among the go-ahead, progressive public universities, recently ranked among the top five public colleges in the north east in terms of research grants and contracts. He was not the least bit surprised when he was short-listed for the position of president.

What did surprise him, however, was the vehemence of the negative reaction from both students and faculty. The Faculty Senate voted unanimously to send a letter of no confidence to the chair of the selection committee—and rather nastily managed to leak it to the press at the same time. When he gave his required public talk about himself and his suitability for the job, he was amazed to find that there was a large protest group among the students attending. They booed when he was introduced by the chairperson of the university council, and as he started to talk, they unfurled posters they had smuggled in which read things like "DON'T LET THE MILITARY INDUSTRIAL COMPLEX DESTROY OUR UNIVERSITY," and "KEEP CALM AND CARRY HIM OFF," and "FENTON'S NOT BAGDAHD," and "NO BOOTS ON OUR GROUND."

They interrupted and heckled, and hissed when he said he was surprised that college students couldn't spell Baghdad. He did his level best to present a reasoned case why both his higher education and his military experiences gave him a unique perspective on the issues facing the US, and he talked a little about the dangers ISIS presented and how the men and women in the armed services were sacrificing much, sometimes making the ultimate sacrifice, to keep America safe. He kept his cool most of the time and repeatedly said he was pleased to see the spirit of debate was alive at CVSU and that he welcomed their exercise of their rights to free speech. He promised he'd listen, as the chief executive, to all of them if he were appointed.

Faculty in the audience were sullen and silent. Most of them felt a bit embarrassed at the rudeness of the student protestors, even though they essentially agreed with them. A few older professors, with grey hair and beards and little bellies hanging over their trouser belts, seemed to be reliving the good old days of Vietnam protests and were waving placards as well. But it was Susan Kraus, the provost, and not the council chairperson, who eventually stood up in the audience, went over to the mike, and in a friendly but firm way requested some civility. She guaranteed the audience a serious question-and-answer session after General Michaels' presentation, but first they had to let him speak. It quietened everyone down, and by the end of his presentation a few of the more conservative professors were beginning to turn to each other and mutter, "He's not so bad after all, we need someone strong in the position, someone who can stick it to the central admin in Albany, and who can persuade the Republican-controlled State Senate to approve more funding for the university."

Somewhat to his surprise, after this reception, Jack Michaels, Lieutenant General, US Army, Retired, DSM, GWTSM, was offered the position, with a five-year renewable contract. The Vice Provost and Dean of the Graduate School, one of the other two candidates, was passed over, despite being popular with faculty—insiders were thought to be lacking vision for new directions. Once that sort of narrative is whispered around, you're done for, no matter how well you have served the university. A humanities dean from a Big Ten university, the third candidate short-listed, had bombed the public interview by suggesting the sciences had become too powerful in most universities and that students were far less interested in STEM majors than the government thought they should be. Michaels was appointed pretty much by default. The

Fenton newspaper, which had liberal leanings, wrote a scathing editorial asserting that if the general truly was the best candidate, the Council should have started a new search.

It was going to be an inauspicious start to a new job: just four months into it, his attempt to consult with faculty about a sensitive security issue seemed to have backfired. Jack was not someone to back down, however. Not for nothing had he been awarded the bizarrely named Global War on Terrorism Service Medal and the genuinely meritorious Distinguished Service Medal. His definition of good leadership was that you found ways to persuade men to do dangerous or unpleasant things that were ultimately good for them and for their unit and for the country. The country was facing threats, and the local security forces needed to be better prepared. Sure, weaponry was not the only issue. Early detection was important—that psychology intern was smart and sensible although it wasn't clear how such a low-ranking person got herself into the meeting. He wasn't convinced semi-automatic rifles were needed. But there had to be some way of appeasing the campus police, and in the end, it should be his decision. Just like in the military, you must take responsibility for your inaction as well as your actions.

When Jack got home, he talked to Tomoko about the meeting. She almost always agreed with him on issues she recognized she knew little about. She had been appalled that there had been controversy over his appointment to Chenango Valley State University. She knew what a good organizer he was and how he thought strategically and for the future. He had ideas about how lesser-known public universities could grow and develop and contribute to modern society. He had some traditional views about discipline, hard work, and loyalty to principles, but he also had lots of progressive attitudes as well. He saw the public universities as being the opportunity for ordinary young people from working and middle-class families to get ahead.

The annual tuition at CFSU was about six thousand dollars a year. It was a bargain. He believed that students should pay this modest amount, not get some sort of free college as a right, which others were advocating. Why should the taxes of working men and women be used to support the young people from families easily able to afford the CVSU tuition, or students goofing off and not attending classes, wasting time and maybe never graduating? He would back scholarships, work-study programs, and low interest loans to make sure people weren't denied college because it was not affordable. He had already called a meeting with the local superintendents to get their thoughts on how to make the promise of college something that would motivate high school students to graduate with decent grades. The drop-out rate in the surrounding rural communities was way too high. A place like CVSU could be an inspiration. What ideas did they have? Campus visits, science fairs run by our distinguished faculty? College prep classes in the schools?

He could also use his military credentials to impress the New York State Senators and US Congress men and women to keep funding Pell Grants. But reasonable tuition costs made young students appreciate what they had. And if they were paying something, they were consumers, not welfare recipients, and they had a right to the best possible education and the right to evaluate faculty, and the university overall.

47

"Consumers have the power of the market place," he explained, and Tomoko agreed. She had heard all this before, but so what?

"Why should the quality of the programs at CVSU be any less than those of the Ivy League? My task, as I see it, is to encourage the faculty to excel, to reward great teaching and research productivity, to provide administrative support so they could get on with being brilliant teachers and not be struggling with poor technology or inadequate library resources, or poor-quality A-V equipment in the lecture theaters. I need a staff of administrators who share that vision, who are hungry for excellence, and who recognize support for faculty and students as their primary goal.

"But Tome, there are many levels of support, from ever-helpful librarians to efficient cleaners, to vigilant security. That's why I want to support Finch and his officers, despite having serious misgivings about guns on campus. I'm not anti-gun. You know I know how to handle firearms. I respect the power they have for good, even if sometimes, too often, used for evil. Hey, do you want another glass of chardonnay?"

Getting up and going to the fridge, he thought about the way the faculty group had just assumed he was on Finch's side, because he had been a general—well, only three stars, but still a major accomplishment. *They* were the sheep—uncritically making facile assumptions about him. He wasn't automatically on Finch's side. That's why it was good Susan had suggested a committee—a good committee could develop a policy that would satisfy everyone. The campus police needed to be prepared and ready for an emergency. But they couldn't be so overt about it, that they generated the very sense of threat and anxiety they were trying to avoid. It was the same delicate way the President and the Secretary of State were dealing with Iran. What was it that Teddy Roosevelt had said?

"Here, hon, 'Speak softly and carry a big stick.' Here's your chardonnay—I've filled the glass quite full because it was the end of the bottle. I didn't want to save a dribble."

"What are you talking about, dear? Who's carrying a big stick? You're losing me."

"Me and Teddy Roosevelt, Tome! Will the committee be smart enough to see that and to make the necessary compromises? If they aren't, I have little choice but to move ahead without them. Because in the end that is what it means to be a leader—you have to be willing to make the unpopular decisions when you know they are for the good of the majority and for the safety of the community."

Tomoko nodded her agreement. He was a thoughtful and decent man. She may not have been the love of his life—or he hers—but she was determined to back him up and to make his life easy. That was love in her book.

"You're the general, sweetie!" she said, "and a lot wiser than your hero, Napoleon!"

"He's not exactly my hero."

"Well, you have a lithograph of him hanging in the study."

"Maybe, but it was done when he was captured and exiled to St. Helena, or Elba or somewhere. He's depicted as all dark and morose. I don't want to end up like that. I'm going to be a success here in Fenton, trust me."

Chapter 6: The Clinic

Katrina Moss left the Valley Garden café and walked briskly to the clinic. She had flat shoes on. She had good legs and didn't need heels, and when she was seeing clients, she tried to wear smart casual clothes and not overdress. She had two clients to see that afternoon, and she regretted having a drink at lunchtime with all those senior faculty types. She delved into her purse and popped a piece of spearmint gum in her mouth; hopefully it would disguise any beer breath. It had been an eventful morning. She had no idea why she had spoken out, and so early, at the meeting, drawing attention to the uncomfortable fact that she was an interloper. Shit, although she was on salary as an intern, she was still only a graduate student, and while her Ph.D. dissertation was all but finished, her degree in clinical psychology would not be awarded until her year-long, full-time internship had been completed to the satisfaction of her supervisors.

The clinic was on the edge of campus and looked like hundreds of other such buildings across modern American public universities emerging in the time of increasingly tight state budgets. It was a single-story, sprawling edifice, built around a square courtyard that had a sort of fishpond-cum-duck pond in the middle. Years ago, its official title was the Counseling and Testing Center, and some of the older faculty in psychology still called it 'The CTC'. But testing was a thing of the past, and its new name was the CVSU Health and Wellness Center: Counseling Services. Now it was a multifunction set-up where students could see a primary care physician, get contraceptive advice, line up for their annual flu shots, and, if emotionally troubled, see either a counseling or a clinical psychologist—usually a trainee. The head of the health services was the only psychiatrist on the staff, Dr. Ali Abidi. There were two intern psychologists that year, both in clinical psychology. Katrina was in the CVSU clinical psychology program, and the other intern had trained downstate.

As Katrina had not yet sat for the state licensing exam, all her work was under close supervision. Dr. Barbara Kennedy, her key supervisor and Director of the APPIC-approved internship program, was unfailingly supportive, even though she had a different orientation. Barbara liked to focus counseling on the client as an individual— 'client-centered' was the common term and Barbara appreciated that humanistic emphasis on the person, not on some mental-health syndrome. Katrina's training program had a very different emphasis. Her professors always talked about clinical work being an applied science, and the importance of using only evidence-based methods. But the clinic's focus on rapport building and a warm, accepting relationship between therapist and client was surely worth learning as well. Katrina felt it was the ideal placement for her, with some suitably challenging clients, not just anxious or depressed undergraduates worried about their relationships. The atmosphere was friendly, focused on professional skills and personal development, and designed to prepare interns for a life of competent, ethical practice. Katrina loved it.

She wasn't quite as enamored of that afternoon's first patient—'client' the Center preferred to call them—a young man named Curtis she had initially seen for an intake interview two weeks earlier. He had missed the previous week's appointment, and frankly Katrina would have been perfectly happy if he had no-showed that day as well, and he could then be sent a polite but firm letter of termination by the receptionist. But Curtis Pierson was there, sitting in the waiting room, jiggling his legs and staring at his cell phone. He was wearing jeans and sneakers, with a scruffy camo jacket over a long-sleeved thick sweatshirt. His hair was cut short and he was clean-shaven, which emphasized his dark complexion. Clearly visible on the side of his neck was a small tattoo of a Dara knot. If anyone asked him about it, he said it was a Celtic symbol for the roots of an oak tree, symbolizing power, endurance and destiny. If it was a girl who asked about it, however, he said it symbolized strength, fortitude, and wisdom. Either way it suited his thin but muscular frame. At high school, other students tended to ignore or avoid him, but at college, girls found him very attractive, in a somewhat enigmatic way.

"Come in Curtis, sorry I'm a few minutes late, I had another important meeting the other side of campus. Let me grab your file from the records room. Sit yourself down—this chair's comfy. Do you want a coffee or a tea or a glass of water?"

He started to take his coat off, and appeared to be searching for a place to hang it.

Katrina noticed and added, "Oh, feel free to hang your jacket on the back of the door here; they keep these offices quite warm."

Katrina had decorated the office as best she could. She had a great 'I Love NY' poster of state wild flowers hanging on one wall, and the two easy chairs were strategically arranged around a low coffee table which had two coasters from a Greenwich Village coffee bar and a mat woven by Onondaga women. Taking an idea from Ronald Reagan, Katrina had a jar of red, white, and blue Jelly Belly beans on her desk. It wasn't there so much for patriotism as for a talking point and something to offer clients when they, or she, were stuck during a session.

Interpersonally, Katrina had been developing a relaxed and cheerful style, and most clients warmed to her right away. Curtis had not. Again, Katrina felt a small pang of discomfort, the same aversion—*dislike if I'm being honest*, she thought to herself, *even if it wasn't professional*—she had felt two weeks ago when he had first presented at the clinic. She hadn't put her finger on exactly why he made her so uncomfortable, but it tilted her towards being more challenging than usual.

"I hope you haven't been ill, have you? You missed last week's appointment, Curtis." It wasn't a reprimand, just a statement of fact. But not to Curtis.

"I had better stuff to do." A put down.

"I'm sure, but just two things to remember—these appointments are for you, not for me, number one, and number two, it would be helpful for us if you call or e-mail the clinic the day before if you have to cancel for whatever reason." Rebuke.

"You didn't give me your e-mail address, and anyway I thought maybe you'd call me to find out if something was the matter." Manipulation.

"Then it was just some sort of test?" Challenge—not a very humanistic inference. "We do sometimes check in with clients, but not typically after only one appointment." Retaliation message: you're not that important to us. "And I never give my personal e-mail information to any client. I gave you a copy of the clinic's procedures and the e-mail address for the reception desk is on it." Further retaliation: follow the rules; you're definitely not that important.

Curtis was silent and Katrina realized she'd come on way too strong. Barbara would have called her on it, if she'd been sitting in, as she occasionally did. Time to back off, maybe even back down.

"Well, Curtis, let's not waste time on what *didn't* happen last week. You're here now, and I'm glad to see you. I want to learn from you much more about why you're here, what concerns you have, and what goals we might set up for our therapy sessions. I got quite a bit of information from you during your first visit, but we didn't pin down what your goals are. I need to get to know you much better so I can be of assistance. You told me a bit about your past, that you grew up in northern Pennsylvania, came up to Binghamton with your mom, but you are now living up here in Fenton, in your own apartment, and you're an undergrad, taking a variety of courses. You haven't declared a major, but..." continued Katrina as she looked down at her laptop and tapped a few keys, "...you're leaning towards something to do with architecture. Have I got it right? You said at first you didn't have any issues, but you were curious as to what counseling might be like. That's fine, but in my experience, something usually triggers a person to come into the Center, something unsettling perhaps, an experience one has not had before—"

"That's it!" Curtis interrupted, "I've never before had the experience of talking to such a cute therapist with such nice legs."

Katrina groaned inwardly. This was going to be a long fifty-five-minute hour. She'd had more than enough experience with difficult clients. She'd even done a practicum with offenders in the Broome County Jail, and some of those men were always trying to hit on her. She paused for a moment, looking Curtis dead in the eye and trying hard to give no sign of being flustered.

"Now Curtis, I think you're a smart young guy. You know perfectly well a remark like that is inappropriate and unhelpful. We're not in some bar or club where you hope to pick up girls. This is a professional relationship. I think you are trying to test me, perhaps see if you can throw me off balance. I'm not sure why you would want to do that, but I'd hazard a guess it's because you have some complex personal issues you came here to address, and you suddenly find it difficult to open up emotionally and tell me honestly what is going on for you. Playing games instead of disclosing your thoughts and feelings is a form of avoidance—quite common for clients actually."

Until Katrina added those last five words, Curtis had been looking at her thoughtfully. But when she said it was a common phenomenon, Curtis startled her by leaping to his feet, glaring at her, and shouting: "But I'm not like any other client!" and stormed out of the room. She heard the glass front door of the center being slammed closed.

Katrina sat where she was. Her heart was beating fast. It was quite unexpected. He was one volatile customer. She immediately wondered where she'd gone wrong. The new, young clinic receptionist, Debbie Kowalski, stuck her head around the door.

"You okay, Kat?" she asked with a worried frown.

"I'm fine thanks Deb. He got upset and left—remind me to call him using the clinic phone in a day or so, and I'll try to get him back in for the same time next week."

"Okay, you have his cell phone number? It should be in my records, if not. I know I shouldn't say anything but I know him. He's weird. We were both in school together, Binghamton High. People avoided him; I think they were scared of him—"

"Thanks Debbie, but don't say any more. You know you must be absolutely discrete and professional—we never gossip about clients. But you could do me a favor and let me know if he contacts the clinic again. I'll tell Barbara what happened. Right now, I've got to calm myself. I've got Bernice coming in at three. I'll just sit here and make some notes, if you'd close the door please."

Katrina crouched over her desk, jotting down a few thoughts on a pad. She tried to remember the exact words Curtis had said when he had lost it—something about not being like others. That could be taken a couple of different ways, like jealousy, or not wanting to be stigmatized, or feeling she had diminished his individuality, but Katrina wrote down 'narcissist?' At that moment, Debbie tapped on her door and, without waiting for a response, opened it and said in a stage whisper: "He's back. He wants to see you. Do you want to see him?"

"Yeah, okay, of course, show him in."

Curtis was calm, acting humble. "I'm sorry," he muttered, "that was childish. I like to stay in control, but I lost it. I've been told I have an anger problem. I know you're trying to help me, and I need it. That's why I came in. And I like you—you're professional. Some therapists wouldn't have been willing to see me when I came back. I've had a lot of shit-assed therapists in my time who didn't like me, but you're different. You seem genuine. I can work with you. I think you're fairly smart—I need someone smart—"

One minute angry as hell, and the next minute sugary sweet. Katrina didn't like it. She interrupted him.

"Look, Curtis, we've lost a bit of time for today. I've got another client coming in..." She glanced at the clock on the wall behind where the clients sat and continued, "...just about fifteen minutes. It seems a pity to get started on heavy stuff. Why don't we make a time for you to come back in a couple of days? And come in an hour or so earlier, as I want to give you a few questionnaires. I'm thinking right now of asking you to complete the MMPI—it's quite a long questionnaire, a whole series of questions, but it will assist me in getting a picture of your personality. We use it to help make diagnoses—"

A dark look crossed Curtis's face. "Diagnosis? You think I'm crazy?"

Katrina shook her head. "We don't call anyone crazy at this center. That's not a word I'd ever use. But people can be depressed, or be stressed, or be struggling with all sort of inner demons." She stopped abruptly; she didn't want to be categorizing him or comparing him to others again. "Hey, don't worry. By diagnosis we just mean trying to get a picture of what makes you tick, what sort of person you are. Everyone is unique and special in their own way. I want to find out what makes you special."

Curtis smiled. "Okay Doc, bring it on. I'll do your questionnaire, and you can analyze me. I also need a prescription filled. I take Tegretol."

Katrina frowned. "You have a seizure disorder?"

"No silly, it helps my mood."

"I'm not a medical doctor. I'll have to refer you to our psychiatrist in the clinic, Dr. Abidi. He's nice."

"Is he an Arab; is he a Muslim?"

"I've no idea. I think he grew up in Cleveland. I think he's an Iraqi–American. Does that bother you? He's a highly-qualified physician."

Curtis shrugged. "No, it's okay, I just like to know. You can't trust most people. Overseas doctors who don't understand or like Americans and are not well trained can be a fuck up, in my experience."

"I can assure you Doctor Abidi is tremendously competent." Katrina wasn't smiling and was beginning to sound testy again.

"Okay, okay, hold your horses, I believe you. Tell the reception lady to give me a time, and I'll be in in a few days to do your little snoopy questionnaire. I'm looking forward to it."

After Curtis left the office, and before Bernice arrived to pour out her recent troubles with her boyfriend, Katrina scribbled 'racist/bigot?' on her notepad.

Chapter 7: Curtis Pierson

Curtis left the campus and went home. His apartment was on the second floor of a creaky Edwardian house on the south side of Fenton. The once respectable family home had long ago been divided into student apartments—two downstairs and one upstairs. The house was dilapidated and in bad need of paint, and the front porch had two broken boards that made it lethal after a disguising blanket of a heavy snowfall—one of the wet 'lake effect' snowstorms common in Fenton. Curtis's apartment was neat and clean. He had almost no furniture—a mattress on the floor in the bedroom, a dining table and three rickety oak chairs, and a metal desk supporting a computer. There was an overstuffed sofa in front of a flat screen TV hanging on the wall.

Curtis rolled a joint and lit it. Dope was one thing that calmed him down. Exercise was another. He had attached a strong steel bar near the top of the bedroom doorframe. He used it regularly for doing chin-ups, which he'd read were better than pull-ups, though easier to do. But he was restless and he couldn't do either with a joint in one hand. He picked up one of his Harbinger power grips and squeezed it once or twice, but couldn't get into his usual intense routine. He couldn't stop thinking about Katrina.

Curtis went to his computer and googled Katrina Moss. Lots of items appeared immediately—some of the photos were of other Katrina's, but Moss's Facebook page (which denied him access) did have a recognizable and rather flattering image of her. She had big brown eyes and a dimple. She could be a model. There was another item on the Internet from the Clinical Studies Program at CVSU about the success of their students last year in gaining approved internships, and a PDF file in the library of her Master's thesis in Psychology, entitled *The relationship between binge eating and self-esteem: Is it mediated by insecure attachment in the pre-pubertal years?* Curtis tried to find an e-mail address for her, but that wasn't so easy. He'd have to subscribe to some sort of service called Peoplephinder, which would cost him twenty-seven dollars. He nearly got out his credit card and signed up, but then he saw it said 'monthly'.

"Fuck you," he said out loud, "I'll think of another way."

He then googled 'Dr. Abidi'. Jeez, there were lots of them. The goddamned Arabs were taking over. He added 'psychiatrist, CVSU' to the search, and sure enough the solemn, aquiline face of Ali Abidi, MD, popped up. There wasn't much other information—he just wasn't important enough or vain enough to have a Wikipedia entry that might have said more about him. He was on LinkedIn, but Curtis was not. He moved on and googled MMPI. There were thousands, nay millions, of entries about the Minnesota Multiphasic Personality Inventory, including a long entry in Wikipedia. Casually scrolling down, he came to an item called 'How to beat the MMPI'. He stopped there immediately because the word 'psychopath' caught his eye. The item was a sort of blog, written by some jerk, which started out with:

If your shrink wants you to complete the MMPI, be super careful. They used the scores to diagnose me as a psychopath, and I have wasted much time trying to get this label changed. The test can be used in many other ways—they might decide you are a schizo, a psychotic, or have what they call a personality disorder. But there is nothing as bad as having it used against you to describe you as a psychopath or sociopath. For you suckers out there, I've done my research and I can now tell you what items you have to look out for. I've listed some below, but I can't be sure that I've nailed all of them. Follow this simple principle: They tend to define you as a psychopath if they decide you have no regard for the feelings of others, and that includes animals. Never admit to being cruel to animals, or enjoying seeing people sad or suffering. Don't report lack of caring for others, and shit like that. They also look for signs of hostility, so never admit to thinking it's impossible for bad people to be rehabilitated, or you believe in capital punishment, that it's okay to get your own back if you've been wronged, or whine that people have treated you unfairly in the past. Being cynical is also a bad sign, so never agree that people are just out for themselves, that people would commit crimes if they thought they could get away with them, or that all guys' major goal in life is to fuck as many women as they can—even though it is true; these assholes judge that to be cynical. Try answering as many of the following items as you can and then scoring one point for 'yes' or 'like me'. If you get more than five points out of twenty, you not just are a psychopath, but you're too stupid to avoid detection. Good luck, and don't ever say you can't get good psychological advice these days!

Curtis was not stupid. He tried the items and got zero out of twenty, and he smiled. He was going to have fun with that Katrina—there'd be no moss gathering on him. He smiled again at his own wit. He smoked another joint, and that made him hungry as hell. He opened a can of chili and ate it all without bothering to heat it. He was feeling good—outwitting people affirmed his superiority. Tomorrow he'd park outside the clinic; he knew there was a designated handicapped spot he didn't mind using, and when Katrina came out—he'd already figured out which was her car—he'd follow her home and find out where she lived.

Chapter 8: The Select Committee

That same afternoon, back in his office and feeling a bit sleepy thanks to the beer, Roger MacDonald, a.k.a. Drain Brain, received an unexpected phone call.

"Hi, Roger, this is Susan, Susan Kraus. I've just finished chatting to the president, and he suggested we ask you to chair that small advisory committee we think we should form on campus security and preparedness. Jack's keen on disaster preparedness; maybe it's his long military experience."

"Thanks Susan, but why me? I'm opposed to guns on campus. I think it is a terrible idea. What about asking Dave Gordon to be the chair? He's got time, and he knows all about risk and bears and stuff."

"Dave is retired, Roger, as you know, and while he doesn't necessarily always want to let go, we need a valued full-time professor whom the faculty and students respect. And as to guns, Jack made it clear to me he's not pushing any agenda—he just wants to be certain that the campus is in support of whatever emergency plans we come up with. To be honest, he was a little critical that I, as Provost, had not already put in place a campus-wide procedure for an active shooter—he said all the universities and high schools have their plans, their lock-down procedures. And he kept telling me he is not pro guns; he just doesn't want us to be sitting here defenseless."

"That sounds like the usual crap about the need for good people with guns."

"Come on Roger, don't be unreasonable. You'd be a good person to get this group together and come up with something sensible. You're not an extremist, and I've often heard you in the Faculty Senate—you listen, you bring contrary ideas together, and you don't antagonize people."

"What you're looking for, then, is some sort of patsy who won't rock the president's boat. But what the heck, I'll do it. Just for you, Susan. It must be difficult having a new boss who's an alpha dog, not like Sarah, rest in peace, whom we all adored."

"Roger, I'm not going to gossip about the senior leadership. Don't underestimate President Michaels or assume you know his attitudes just because he was a general. He's a complex man, and I think he wants to be liked—don't we all?—and to do a good job here at the university. It will take him a while to understand the culture of a university—it's so different from a military unit with a rigid chain of command. Give him some time and some leeway before you judge. We must all get along, and that's why I'm very pleased you've accepted the role—it's just for a year as chairperson of the new Security Committee. That's its name. Let's talk about members. I've got some ideas…"

Susan and Roger chatted back and forth about suitable names. She raised Ali Abidi as a possibility.

"President Michaels suggested him. Neither of us know him very well. He keeps a low profile. I wasn't even involved directly with his appointment. It came down from the system Chancellor in Albany, apparently direct from the Governor, so

I've always assumed he was some sort of ally in Iraq and that our country owed him. I've heard only good things about his work, and the CTC is flourishing under his leadership. Why don't you go talk to him rather than calling him? Since he didn't come to the meeting, he needs a bit more background."

"You should invite him, Susan, and then he can't say no."

"Roger, you're a good chap, but you know nothing about campus politics—or people, apparently!" She was chuckling on the phone. "I don't want to force people onto the committee, I want them to volunteer, and it will be your committee, not mine. I'd want Dr. Abidi to know that, so you have to talk to him."

"You didn't mind forcing *me* to be the chairperson," Roger grumbled, but Susan just snorted lightly.

"Thanks Roger for doing this. I think it's important. I can't imagine anything untoward happening in this peaceful place, but I'd kick myself if it did and we hadn't been at least somewhat ready and prepared. And we need the campus police on board, not resentful and angry because we're not taking them seriously. One of their top guys needs to be on the committee—I'll leave that to you. Thanks again Roger, I appreciate it." The provost hung up.

Two days later, Roger was sitting in Ali Abidi's sparse office. There were two framed certificates on the wall, one his M.D. from Yale University Medical School, and the other, in Arabic, from the University of Baghdad—the one English phrase read 'Specialization in Psychiatry'. Below them, just taped to the wall, was a copy of his annual New York State medical license. Next to the gray metal desk was a lateral filing cabinet. A university-issue bookcase had a small selection of textbooks, some on general medicine, but most on topics like child and adolescent psychiatry, psychotropic pharmacology, and an old copy of the *Diagnostic and Statistical Manual of Mental Disorders*. Even though he had been with the university some years, it didn't look like he'd settled in or made his office personal in any way. On the opposite wall, however, was a poster of pebbles stacked on a beach, with the words 'Tranquility' underneath, and under that the quotation: "*We need more peacemakers, not revolutionaries…with these, we create a heaven on earth.*"

"Nice poster," Roger said.

"It was here in the office when I moved in," Ali Abidi replied, and Roger, feeling that was dismissive—after all he was only trying to make small talk—decided instantly he didn't much like the man. He focused on his mission.

"The provost has asked me to chair a small committee on campus safety and security. The idea came from the meeting the president had called. I know you weren't there, but I feel it would be crucial to have a person such as yourself with a strong background in mental health to review or suggest any processes we might set up within the university community."

"I got a short briefing from Miss Moss, our clinical psych intern, but she didn't offer any details. Is your committee being set up by the provost or by the president?"

"Well, Susan Kraus contacted me, but I'm sure it's designed to support President Michaels."

"Unfortunately, Doctor MacDonald, you'll have to count me out. I'm the only psychiatrist in this health center, and my hands are full. I'm not an authority on violence or prediction, and I'm sure you will realize there is a certain amount of anti-

Middle-East feeling around here. I was born in Iraq. I'm not a Muslim, I'm not religious at all, but I hear a lot of anti-Muslim sentiment—not so much on campus, but on the local radio stations, even the student newspaper. I would not be a good person for your committee, although I applaud your efforts and your sincerity. Just don't involve me. Let me know if the Center here can help in anyway. I know some of the counselors, especially, are keen to have more sensitivity groups aimed at communication and skills for co-existence and celebration of diversity—you can tell this from that poster you admired."

Roger made no attempt to dissuade the good doctor. It was funny, he thought, sitting in a therapy room, that at that instant he felt *he* was doing the analysis and not the other way around. Roger was a gentle sort of man, with a good sense of humor and a good sense of the absurd. He had learned not to take himself too seriously, and at the same time he was not one to boast or stand out or push his views; he liked the description 'A mild-mannered man'. That suited him. But it also allowed him, in his passive way, to become a good observer of human foibles, and he did rather pride himself on his ability to sense someone's feelings. And at this moment in their interaction, he sensed Dr. Abidi was feeling quite uncomfortable—why, he did not know. His instinct was that being an immigrant was always a difficult role, and at this precise time in American history and politics, it was a particularly difficult one, especially for an Arab. Not surprising he didn't want to stick his neck out. Roger respected that. He was about to accept the doctor's declining the doubtful honor of serving on a likely to be useless committee, and make his departure as courteously as possible, when Dr. Abidi interrupted his thoughts by saying,

"By the way, Miss Moss, who represented this clinic at the so very important hush-hush meeting, wouldn't tell me what it was about. She said she had promised not to tell anyone, even me, even though I had originally been invited to it."

He paused, perhaps hoping Roger would spill the beans. But as Roger said nothing, Abidi went on, "Well, at least you know she's loyal and discrete. Better ask her to serve on your secret—I mean security—committee."

Roger ignored the sarcasm and nodded his agreement: "She was indeed appropriate, which is a credit to your clinic here. But now I should go and let you get on with your work."

Strolling back to his office, Roger was mulling over both the conversation and the possible composition now of the Security Committee and how likely it was he could keep both the fact of the committee and its mission secret for long. He did not notice a thin, wiry, athletic-looking young man scurrying past him towards the Counseling Center. Curtis Pierson was on his way to be administered the Minnesota Multiphasic Personality Inventory, for which he was well-prepared.

Sitting in his office, Roger made a few phone calls and sent out a couple of e-mails. By the end of the day, he had the membership tied down. He obviously needed the head of security, Chief of Campus Police Gary Finch, the man who'd been itching to get his hands on some heavy-duty fire-power. For balance, Roger had decided to focus on people who had attended the original meeting and whose opinions he was reasonably sure of. Marcia Kastanowicz would be a good choice—Roger was always more comfortable with people in the sciences. They didn't waffle as much, and they respected evidence and facts. On the other hand, Phil Cohen had a background in strategic studies and seemed to be aware of President Michaels' scholarly record—that might be useful. Karl Goga was a sensible pick—a campus safety officer could also represent the non-academic staff, and he had lots of inside knowledge of the campus, the labs, and general safety issues. Roger realized that basically he had selected his lunch-time companions, but that was okay—he knew them and he was comfortable with them and their attitudes, and they weren't extreme left-wing crazies trying to recapture their rebellious youths, like some of the older faculty. In fact, he knew Karl Goga liked hunting and was certainly a gun-owner.

Finally, after a long pause and lots of internal dialog, he sent Katrina Moss an invitation. If he was questioned about it, he would say, truthfully, that she had been nominated by Dr. Abidi. Roger liked Katrina and tried to ensure that wasn't influencing his judgment. The key thing, he decided, was she represented the student community, or could claim to do so, and also she would be another woman. He needed the gender balance on his ad hoc committee.

By six-thirty that evening, he had all the members in place and a couple of meeting dates, times, and locations set up, and he went home satisfied with his work. He was sure they could drag out the discussion of automatic assault-style weapons for the campus police for a couple of semesters, in the time-honored tradition of all university hot-button issues. By then, the excitement would have died away and there would be some other problem to distract the president.

In the meantime, the committee could do a few useful things. Gary Finch wanted an expanded budget for his Safe Ride Program that had been trialed recently and which deployed their squad cars rather than simply escorting students from some late-night lab experiment to their cars in the remote student parking lot. They could legitimately advocate for that expenditure—everyone would agree. And they could develop a more coordinated communication plan for the unlikely event of a shooter on campus. Maybe a student-wide text alert. That was a no brainer and a bit like a community preparedness plan for a major earthquake, another event that was highly improbable. Back at home, Roger felt quite pleased with himself, so he opened a good bottle of red wine, found a heat-and-serve lasagna in the freezer, and settled down to watch an episode of *The Americans* on television.

Chapter 9: Stalking

It was almost dark. Curtis sat in his car on the opposite side of the road from where Katrina had parked and then walked down the small side lane to the back of a large house. It was a few miles outside of Fenton. The house looked like it had once been a farmhouse, but now it was considerably updated and modernized. Behind the house, partially hidden by fir trees, was a large wooden barn, and Curtis had just been able to see a flash of light as Katrina opened a door into the barn. Huh, this was where she lived. Quite isolated. Excellent. The only drawback was that with it being on a country road, there were virtually no other cars around. Next time he would park much further away and sneak towards the house—no one would notice that, just another guy taking an evening stroll, or walking his dog. Curtis snickered, thinking how he might carry a leash and a little blue plastic dog poop bag. Or maybe he wouldn't bother.

Katrina loved her apartment. She had found it when she started grad school at CVSU, and it had become the envy of her friends. It was a converted barn that the Richardsons, who owned the main house, had modified for their son who was now in California. The upstairs, which had once been for storing hay, was just one large room with a small kitchen and a bathroom along one side. Above these was a sleeping loft, accessed via a sturdy wooden ladder. Downstairs, where the cows had once been milked, there was a blue front door leading into a vestibule Mr. Richardson had decorated in a kitschy way with old farm implements—the spoils of many a local yard sale. The rest of the downstairs space the owners used as the garage for their two cars; it also had the furnace that blasted warm air to the upper level. What was most delightful was that the entire far wall upstairs—the long side of the original barn—had been converted into a massive picture window. It was too large for drapes or blinds, but in any case, Katrina wouldn't have closed any—she loved to lie in bed and look out at the huge blue spruce trees, which were magnificent in the winter with piles of soft snow on their branches.

Curtis waited about half an hour after Katrina got home and then cautiously entered the yard, following the path she had taken. He hoped they didn't have a dog. Most people living the rural life did, so he had come prepared—in one pocket was a canister of pepper spray, in the other a Ziploc baggie with some chunks of cheap stewing beef. Curtis had a low opinion of pet dogs. He only liked those breeds that were bred for toughness and aggression—the Dobermans and the Pitbulls. A juicy pile of steak wouldn't deter *them* from attacking, whereas any ordinary domestic breed would instantly prefer gobbling down meat than chasing an intruder. But there were no dogs.

There were also no windows on the side with the blue door. However there seemed to be a glow of light on the other side, so he edged his way around the barn to the back of the yard. Needing to stay out of the shaft of soft light coming from the barn's big windows, Curtis found himself walking on soft ground, Was it a lawn, a garden bed, or just old pine needles? He couldn't be sure. But once he had worked his way to the far side, with the windows, he stopped thinking about what was under his feet. Bingo! He'd hit pay dirt. Crouching in among some low bushes, he could now see right into Katrina's well-lit studio apartment.

It was a bit too high to see Katrina, however. He looked around for a possible tree. The spruces were too dense and the silver birches were too straight up and down. Happily, for him, he found a locust with spreading branches he could climb. It was quite far back, and by the time he had a clear view into the barn, he realized that next time he had to bring binoculars. However, at that moment, Katrina was quite clearly visible coming out of the bathroom. Damn, she had a robe on. Then Curtis's heart pounded—she was taking off the robe and putting on pajama bottoms and an old T-shirt. There was no need for her to worry about standing naked in her apartment—there was nothing outside but trees. Curtis shoved his hand into his jeans to touch himself, but his excitement was so high and his heart was beating so fast, he wasn't hard. "Come on Katrina, take your time with those PJs," he whispered out loud.

She didn't, but he had seen enough to be able to jerk off to his image of this wonderful sight later that night. Katrina went back into the bathroom, maybe to brush her teeth, and then he saw her nimbly climb the ladder into the sleeping loft. He waited expectantly for another ten minutes. It looked like she was reading. Then she abruptly switched off all lights, and the show was over. There wasn't much of a moon, but in whatever light there was, Curtis knew he was now potentially as visible to her as she had been to him. Even though he was in dark clothes, he decided not to move down from the tree for about fifteen minutes. Surely she'd be asleep by then.

When he finally felt it safe to leave and he got back to the car, he was still shaking. He was parked on a slight slope, and so he put the car in neutral and rolled down the road a little way before starting the engine. *Oh, what a fucking success,* he thought to himself, *just as I pictured in the therapy room, Katrina Moss has great tits.* There she had stood, stark naked, revealed for his pleasure. What a miracle. And that would not be the last time he would see her like that. For every free evening he had, this was going to be his new entertainment.

Back in his apartment, Curtis went to a steel cabinet and unlocked it. Inside was a hunting rifle with a telescopic sight, and Curtis's pride and joy, a Glock G43 9mm pistol: *Designed for confidence; fits every lifestyle,* says their ad, *proudly manufactured in Smyrna, Georgia.* Which wasn't entirely true, since most of the parts were made in Austria. Stuck on the back of his cabinet was a bumper sticker, reading *Liberals: The people your Founding Fathers warned you about.* At the bottom of the cabinet, wrapped in an oily cloth was a single-action Colt revolver, the Lightning .38, with a 6-inch barrel, made in 1904, but a classic model which had been in use since 1877. It had cost Curtis over six hundred dollars a couple of years back. He didn't use it. He had tried it out once at a firing range and it worked, but proper ammo was hard to get, so mostly he just took it out, cleaned it lovingly, and practiced quick draws and spinning it on his trigger finger. He kept all six chambers in the cylinder empty so he could practice cocking the hammer with his other hand. He knew he was being childish, but the sense of power, of risk, of being a serious miscreant outlaw somewhere in the badlands gave him a lot of pleasure. He'd bought it from a friend of a friend who'd purchased it on the Internet, and he didn't have a license for it, although he did have an owner's license for the pistol. In New York State, he did not need a permit to buy or own the hunting rifle now that he was over 21.

Curtis checked everything in the cabinet, including some boxes of ammunition, and it calmed him down. He felt powerful, able to defend himself. In deer season, hunting gave him a sense of excitement, not unlike what he had felt outside Katrina's apartment; sitting in the tree wasn't very different from sitting behind a tree watching a deer coming closer and closer. On Katrina's questionnaire, he had been careful to state his love for animals. That was true he thought—he always waited silently for the deer to come whisker close so he could bring it down with one clean shot. That was the sign of manhood, he reasoned, not blasting off ten rounds through the trees and bushes at the bobbing white tail of a snorting, terrified, running deer. And while he waited for that one clean shot, the tension rose steadily, just like it would when waiting in the dark for Katrina to emerge naked from her bathroom. Relief from that tension was the most rewarding feeling in the world.

Chapter 10: Psychopathology

Katrina was sitting with her clinical supervisor, Dr. Barbara Kennedy, for their weekly review of her case load.

"I've got some serious concerns about a client I've seen three times now plus one testing session where I administered the MMPI, so four times altogether. The first session was frustrating. I had a hard time pinning down why he had come to the clinic. I got a sense his main reason was to persuade me to get Ali to write a prescription for him. Apparently, he'd come in one day asking to see a doctor because he needed a mood stabilizer he'd been on for a while. Ali quite rightly said that before he would okay a refill, he needed more time to get to know him, but since his diary was full for the next few days, the patient could see me instead, and I'd make a recommendation for medication. When he saw me, he was evasive and shifty, and we didn't get far; I felt uncomfortable. You know how hard it is to identify a gut feeling like that! I just felt he was a bit off.

"He's a good looking young guy, quite dark skinned, short hair. His name's Curtis. He keeps fit, he says, and it shows. He dresses like the locals you see at the mall, and acts self-assured. Said he didn't have to study too hard because he tended to be smarter than the other students in class, so I accessed his academic record and sure enough, he mostly has A's or A+'s across a wide variety of subjects. There doesn't seem to be much focus to his course choices. I asked him about his major, and he said he was always looking for something that would be sufficiently challenging. Recently he had found architectural studies quite interesting, but he expressed a lot of hostility towards the faculty—apparently, an advisor in that department had told him it was unlikely he had any real aptitude. Curtis then said if he had a chance one dark night, he would get back at that prick, and a baseball bat across his kneecaps would be his just deserts. I must have looked startled, but he just smiled and said, 'I'm only kidding Kat. Can I call you Kat?' I said 'No, no one calls me Kat except people who've known me for a long time.' Well, he must have resented that because most of the time now he calls me 'Doctor Moss' and then immediately corrects himself and sneers: 'Oh, I keep forgetting, you're not yet a doctor, you're just a student like me.'

"He missed the next session, but came back the following week. I made a totally innocuous remark that proved to be some kind of a trigger I don't understand, because right in the middle of the session he leaped out of the chair and ran out of the room, slamming the door. He came back later, but there was no time to carry on. I just arranged to administer the MMPI. I've scored it, Barbara, and it makes no sense. I know you're not big on making diagnoses from test scores and you don't like diagnostic labels, but I sure expected him to show strong features of being a psychopath—you know, high Pd (Psychopathic deviate) score. But that doesn't show up at all. On the other hand, he has quite high scores on Social Desirability and the Lie items, so maybe the whole test is suspect.

"The next two sessions were weird. He came in acting completely different. He was solicitous, asked how I was feeling because I looked a little tired. He sat as close to me as he could, and he kept looking at me like we were on a date—intense eye contact, and he also said, 'You've got very pretty eyes, Miss Moss.' I tried hard not to show it, but I'm sure I was a bit rattled. He's creepy, and I know that isn't a diagnosis, but he was so unctuous. He said he'd been reading about transference and wondered if I believed in it. I gave him the usual CBT spiel about not accepting those Freudian ideas, and he replied surely it was true that patients and therapists could have feelings for each other. Look, Barbara, I've got the session tape of what happened next—"

"Did you get his signed consent?"

"Sure, I got it the first session. Told him I had a supervisor who would need to know what was happening in our sessions. You know how worried some clients are about that, but he seemed delighted. He said that was wonderful because it meant two high-powered professionals were interested in him. Not his precise words, but that was the gist—he seemed to want to show off, and I think that is one reason he throws out such odd things—I often feel he is trying to shock me, or at least get me off balance. Listen to this exchange. She switched on her digital recorder:

Katrina: I've checked on some possible times Dr. Abidi can see you for a medication review, but I can't promise he will want to continue you on Tegretol. We need to have a better understanding of your needs.

Curtis: I heard he was in Iraq with the US Army, but he doesn't show up on any Internet sites. I googled him.

Katrina: Why did you do that Curtis?

Curtis: Because I like to know things. How do you know he's not ISIS, just waiting to attack us?

Katrina: Come on, you don't believe that, someone as smart as you. Why were you looking him up?

Curtis: Curiosity. The same reason you looked me up on the university system.

Katrina: I did not.

Curtis: Now you are just lying—I don't mind, honestly I don't, I'd have done the same, just as I looked at your Facebook page. But I know you accessed my grades. I filed a privacy status request a few days ago, and I was told only legitimate university faculty can look at a student's records and that there has been only one such search last week. They designed the system to protect students.

Katrina: Okay, that's true. I looked up your student *academic* record. I have the authority. I was just interested in making sure I had your home phone number or cell phone in case I had to reach you. I'm not interested in your grades.

Curtis: That sounds like total bullshit to me, but it isn't important. I want to know what you know about Dr. Abidi. You just can't be too careful. Look at Dr. Hasan—

Katrina: Who?

Curtis: Major Nidal Hasan. *He* was a psychiatrist too, and a major in the army and he shot and killed thirteen soldiers right in the middle of Fort Hood. Now he's on death row. The guys who took him down must have been lousy shots not to have killed him there and then. If I'd been there he wouldn't have taken out more than one guy. And he was fuckin' born in America too, and incidentally, Dr. Abidi was *not* born or grew up in Cleveland. He was born in Iraq. That much I could find out from other sources. And how the other psychiatrists Hasan was working with couldn't figure out the guy was looney tunes, I don't know. Psychiatry isn't an exact science like other branches of medicine, is it? More a way of controlling people with drugs. Maybe that's why he wants to review my meds. What do you think?

Katrina: Curtis, you are being particularly tangential and talkative today. Is there something else going on for you right now that's bothering you?

Here, Barbara Kennedy interrupted. "Stop the tape, Katrina, and let's deconstruct this. Reflect on an important question. Where were you going with this? You were quite challenging a couple of times, I thought. You've said some rather negative things about this client, and now I'm feeling from the tape that you were on the defensive. You used critical terms to his face, like 'tangential', though I thought he was answering your question. Does he scare you? Were you feeling anxious? You don't seem to be letting the session flow over any obstacles, like a stream drifting over rocks; no, you seem to want to constrict the current—to direct the flow. But if you decide on the direction, you don't know where the client might have led you. Right? And I don't think you have a good working relationship established yet. The session seems like a cat and mouse game and you're the mouse, not the 'Kat', excuse the bad pun. It's okay to be uncomfortable, but if you are so unsettled by this particular client, we have to process that a bit."

Katrina was silent. This was the kind of moment when she disliked the way humanistic psychotherapists talked about issues. She was the normal person here, and Curtis seemed to have a significant disorder. But Barbara was the supervisor, and she was there to learn.

"Okay, I confess, as I have already, he makes me uncomfortable. But I don't think I'm treating him unprofessionally. At the very least I'm sure he has a personality disorder—I know it's easy to pin that label on clients we don't like, but there is something off about him. It's not a professional word, but he's creepy. The MMPI results were inconclusive. I was sure he was going to show up as a psychopath. I think the signs are there: superficial, socially manipulative, intelligent but not insightful, has contempt for others, high and unjustified self-esteem. He doesn't seem to have friends or engage in typical student activities. He's something of a loner as far as I can judge from what he's told me about his day to day activities and habits.

"And I think I'm managing the sessions as best as possible. My plan for the moment is to get him to trust me enough to disclose what's on his mind. Anxious, yes, I guess I am. A couple of years back, I took a course on forensic clinical psychology with Dr. Milsop in Psychology, and we went into a few cases of young men who have become mass shooters. We looked especially closely at Cho at Virginia Tech and at the Aurora shooting. James Holmes killed twelve and injured seventy but was a patient of a psychiatrist at the time.

"The reason we studied the details was that in both cases there were signs that were missed by mental health professionals who had been in contact. Since then I've become massively wound up about the possibility this might happen to me—that I'm not sufficiently perceptive to recognize the danger signs. That was what Curtis was talking about in that segment I just played you—why didn't Major Hasan's medical colleagues see what was going on? I think I've become hyper vigilant and not in a good way—it's sort of an obsessional worry. Will I be the person who misses the obvious signs?"

"That shows terrific insight Katrina, exactly what I'd hope for in an intern at your level. By recognizing your anxiety in this relationship, you will be better able to make more balanced judgments. You certainly didn't use good rapport-building, and open-ended interview techniques are just as much part of cognitive-behavior therapy as they are of my orientation. Think about the situation from a power and control perspective. Here you are asking him what I would consider trivial questions about his daily activities instead of looking at the bigger picture, perhaps the way Foucault might do. We should look at the situation from a new lens, starting with your relationship with yourself.

"You have expressed ambivalence—you want to accept him and be compassionate, but you have suspicion and anxiety; the latter has probably been imposed on you as a woman by male teachers who emphasize domination in all relationships, including the therapeutic bond. You used the word managing the session. But I wasn't accusing you of not being in control, but the opposite—of not allowing it to find its natural course. I wonder if you are being over-controlling in order to reduce the unpredictability of his style. The Western, male, scientific narrative privileges certain ways of relating to clients. As the mental health expert, you are assuming power and Curtis is resisting it. And I don't see how lying to him will help build trust.

"I think to understand him better, you need to drop the tools of patient domination, such as the MMPI and the Diagnostic and Statistical Manual—what's the DSM number up to now, is it five? Try being more accepting. Approach him on equal ground, be more overtly accepting, encouraging him not to resist you but to open himself in a safe context. Remember he knows, or is aware, that his voice is being subjected to critical analysis—your subjective definition of what's abnormal or what's permitted.

"Let's just hypothesize for a moment that he has had a long period of being dominated by others, an abusive father, for example, or a manipulative mother. Didn't you say he asked about transference? That's unusual for a client; perhaps he recognizes he's approaching you like harsh authority figures from the past and he knows that's unhelpful. Foucault might call you a polemical practitioner because you start with categories like diagnoses into which you are trying to fit this young man."

Dr. Kennedy could see the look of confusion on Katrina's face, and she decided to back off—these students trained in the so-called scientist practitioner framework had a hard time understanding the importance of the implicit discourse of their practice. She softened her position; after all, in this supervisory relationship, she too should be careful to practice reciprocal elucidation, letting Katrina herself discover this level of understanding.

"Let's make this a bit more practical. What I'm suggesting is you suspend your need for diagnosis, labeling, or goal-setting, and focus instead on building a meaningful relationship with Curtis. One that's not a male-style battle for dominance, but one allowing him to reflect, not challenge. Self-question, rather than second-guess your interrogatory demands."

Katrina was silent. Five years of graduate training had drummed into her a high regard for the very Western scientific discourse that Barbara was implicitly trying to dismantle. It was unsettling, but that's what supervision was all about. That's how you grow as a therapist, isn't it? Being reflective, being challenged? After four sessions with Curtis, there was no doubt she was getting nowhere, and she was frustrated. Much as she disliked Barbara's way of tying the whole issue to some sort of feminist philosophizing, she knew she could at least try a different way. And Barbara, highly experienced after twenty years of practice at the counseling center, didn't seem the least bit perturbed by Curtis's clinical presentation. Maybe she had been overly influenced by her own dread of missing the next crazy shooter on a college campus.

"I'll try, Barbara. I understand what you're saying, and I'll focus on a quite different approach to the therapeutic alliance. After all, an alliance implies reciprocal roles, doesn't it?"

For her next session with Curtis, Katrina did some preparation, making notes for herself. Knowing she was still extremely wary, she decided she might make some headway by asking Curtis about three things she had noticed. One was his e-mail address, another was his out of the blue question about transference, and the third was an off-hand remark he'd made about his mother being a 'warden'. Katrina had taken the latter remark figuratively, but perhaps it was literal. She also realized that given Curtis's apparent constant interest in her—thankfully her Facebook page was available only to a few designated friends—she might try the tactic of being more self-disclosing.

That, she was not going to mention to Barbara. She knew, by calling it a tactic rather than honest sharing, she'd risk getting another few minutes of Foucault, and she'd had quite enough of that already. She smiled, realizing that while she was going to try her supervisor's approach, she had not been converted—they didn't share 'lenses' and probably never would.

"Hi Curtis," she began the next session, "I'm pleased to see you. I've had a rough day with some academic work, and I'm looking forward to us having a good conversation this afternoon. See? No notes, no jotting down things on my iPad. I've got some questions, but you might have some too."

"What, no clever little diagnostic tricks today, looking for symptoms?"

"Touché. I know I've been doing that a bit too much. But hey, here's a question. Tell me about your e-mail address. I first used your campus e-mail which is cpierson@cvsu.edu, but recently you sent a message to the clinic from a personal address which was prisoncurseit@gmail.com."

Curtis smirked, looking at her quizzically. Katrina continued. "It didn't take me long to figure out 'prison, curse it' was a perfect anagram of your name, but I wondered if you had any personal experience of prison, or someone in your family, perhaps?"

Curtis sat up in his chair, delighted. "That's what I mean Katrina, you're so smart. We're a good match. There's no point playing Kill Shot Bravo with a dummy."

"What on earth's that?"

"It's just a video game. Super popular. It's a shooter game. You battle all sorts of bad guys including drones, exo-suits, mechs, other snipers—"

"Good God, I've no idea what you're talking about, but it sounds dreadful."

"Just harmless fun. That game requires strategy and tactics. I'm a very high scorer."

"Hmm, I'm sure, but I'm not playing, remember, only connecting. Tell me about prison."

"I've never been to prison. Prison's for losers who've gotten caught. But my mother went to prison. She died in prison. Hung herself."

Katrina searched his face for his usual mocking expression, but for the first time ever, she thought she saw genuine emotion. Did he actually have feelings?

"I thought you said that until recently you had been living in an apartment near the bowling alley on Riverbank Parkway across the Chenango, and your mom was the manager there, and she blamed your dad's death on the stress of unemployment." Katrina could simply not disguise the suspicion in her voice—Curtis was undoubtedly a pathological liar.

"That's my adopted mom. I was talking about my real mother. I was in foster care when my real mother went to prison. My foster mom is Gladys Pierson. She adopted me."

"What was your real, your birth mom's name?" She thought this question might catch him out.

"I'd rather not say. And anyway, it is protected by court order. I'm Curtis Pierson now."

The conversation moved on sluggishly—not the free flow that Barbara Kennedy envisaged. Katrina muttered sympathy for Curtis's birth mother, whatever her story might be, and Curtis asked her a bit about her own family—back to being overly curious. Normally Katrina would have deflected such questions, but she had Barbara's admonitions still ringing in her ears. The session ended with Curtis looking pleased and a little smug; and he commented, as he left Katrina's office, that that was the best session he'd ever had. Katrina smiled and nodded, but she felt the exact opposite. She was tense, and knew she hadn't handled their session well at all.

Chapter 11: Committee Progress

Roger went to talk to the provost, Professor Susan Kraus. She had sent a testy e-mail saying she hadn't heard anything at all after he had reported the final membership of his committee. A meeting would be helpful.

"I'm happy to fill you in on progress, Susan; it will be a short meeting. There isn't any."

"Oh dear, why not? Jack will be breathing down my neck any minute."

"There are two reasons, I think. One is I made a mistake by stacking the deck. Basically, everyone on the committee, except Chief Finch of course, is dead set on not expanding the availability of guns on campus. And although I try my best to look at all sides and encourage reasonable debate, some of the members are getting a bit carried away. Phil Cohen I always thought to be wise and thoughtful—maybe it's the beard—but he's a bit of a hothead underneath it all. He keeps saying he doesn't mind guns in southern Baptist churches (apparently there's a bill being discussed in Mississippi) because then they'll all shoot each other. Not helpful.

"And on the other side, Finch is an alarmist. He's been interacting much more with the Fenton police and now, he says, he's in touch with some guy in the FBI. They all tell him there is an increase in jihadi 'chatter'—honestly, I don't know where they get these weird terms from—in the Southern Tier region, and that we have quite a flood of new immigrants. I mentioned it was the 'flood' of new immigrants to the Endicott-Johnson shoe factory that created this entire region, and he said well yes, but they were Italians and Poles and good people like that. I wouldn't go so far as to say he's a racist, but he sure shares some of the local suspicions about Muslims.

"To make matters worse, he keeps describing our campus as a 'soft target'. I asked him what that meant, although I had a fair idea, and he explained a college campus was the very place for a terrorist attack as no one knew how to defend themselves, and his own police force had been emasculated. 'Chemically castrated, drip by drip' were his exact words. His whole argument is that if they were all properly armed then they would suddenly be a hard target and the terrorists would look elsewhere. His conclusion was that if the campus police open-carried semi-automatic assault weapons, it would be far safer because it would be a simple deterrent—like nuclear missiles. The whole committee laughed hysterically at this point, and I had a hard time getting the discussion back to any sort of serious business. I wish you'd appointed someone else, I've always liked a quiet life, free of conflict and displays of testosterone."

The provost looked at him quizzically. "I feel for you, I do. But you're sensible and you're solid—I mean in temperament. You're the right academic for the job. But maybe we could find another member who is more pro-guns and still sensible—"

"That's a contradiction in terms if I ever heard one. But it's not a matter of being pro or anti-guns. I put Karl on because he's an avid hunter. He's not a member of the NRA, but he is a member of Gun Owners' Association of America. I think

Katrina—gosh, she's brilliant—hit it right on the head in one of our meetings when she said the debate was not about guns but about perception of risk, of threat. That people who tended to be suspicious and distrustful and have a low opinion of the innate decency of people, especially those different from themselves, were the ones in favor of taking precautions and protecting themselves. I think she nailed it. I used to think the guns debate was simply between the right-wing and the left-wing, but now I see it as more a matter of intolerance of fear and uncertainty. Katrina said that became obvious when 'stand your ground' legislation was introduced in some states. It was psychological code for 'don't be scared'. I think she's so perceptive." Roger's face lit up, and Susan noticed.

"You're right, she is, but don't put too much on her young shoulders. She's only a student, not a tenured professor. We can't be over-relying on her. Couldn't you get Doctor Abidi to be on the Security Committee?"

"I tried hard. He declined."

"Hmm. Well, let's think about one other member to balance things out a bit. How about having an African American? I should have suggested it earlier. What about Tonya Evans?

"The diversity person?"

"Her title is Chief Diversity Officer. I believe your buddy Dave Gordon has been working with her on Title IX issues, but I learned the other day, which I hadn't realized, that before she got her MA in Sociology, she was a police officer up north somewhere. She represents the black students, and she must know all about guns. Yet presumably, she's also likely to be concerned about gun violence, the way it has affected the black community."

"Will you ask her?"

"No, you have to, as I've told you before. But you can say it was my recommendation. I'm sort of her boss. Sound her out just a little bit before you make a commitment, and remember the specific issue that has Jack and Gary Finch all fired up— ooh, bad choice of words—is the formal assault rifle request. Jack's going to have to make a decision soon. I'll also let Jack know we're thinking of adding Tonya."

When Roger managed to reach Tonya Evans on her cell phone sometime later, and started to talk about a special committee related to security on campus, he was flabbergasted—not too strong a word, he thought to himself later—at her friendly response.

"Sure, Professor MacDonald, I know all about it. President Michaels has already contacted me and said you might be calling. He was enthusiastic. He knows I was a police officer in Rochester. I thought he must have been looking at my personnel file, but then he reminded me I'd met him once when he was at the college up in Brockport. I think he's terrific, just the kind of firm leader we've needed here for a while. He's supportive of black students and faculty. After he was appointed down here, we had lots of discussions about what he could do to increase ethnic diversity on campus and to make sure the black students didn't have any grievances. I think maybe he'd been alarmed by the level of protests and disruption on some of the other colleges. But whatever his motives, I was pleased to have a sense of direct communication, because there are some volatile black students here."

Roger tried to recover his composure. Goddamned President Michaels already interfering and pulling strings. Shit.

"But wouldn't they be especially concerned about gun violence? I'm not making a judgment here, just thinking about powerful movements like Black Lives Matter."

"That's my point. Students like that are disruptive. They're immature. They don't achieve greater equality or better academic outcomes for black students, and they disrespect the police. President Michaels was encouraging when I said my mission was to ensure black students on this campus are not side-tracked with useless political issues and to focus on making sure they have academic opportunities and fairness."

Roger clenched his teeth. *Our African–American diversity officer is anti-black. Probably a Republican—there have been a few prominent black people recently who've become darlings of the right.* But it was too late to back off.

"Well Tonya, it sounds like you are agreeing to be on the Security Committee. Welcome aboard. I'll send you an e-mail about the next meeting time. I'm sure your perspective will be welcomed by the group, and I look forward to your counsel." *Oh, liar, liar, pants on fire,* he said to himself.

Chapter 12: Conversations

Dr. Abidi walked into Katrina's office. She was eating lunch and hastily put down her egg-salad sandwich on wheat bread, and wiped her mouth with a paper napkin.

"Sorry Ali, you've caught me with my mouth full. What can I do for you?"

"It's about your patient, Curtis. I finally got to see him for the medical consult. I read your note in his file that you were withholding any diagnosis for now in an attempt to establish better rapport, but my impression is that he's borderline. He seems to me to be labile and emotionally uncontrolled; he has mood swings, and reports chronic feelings of emptiness. He said he never uses marijuana. I wanted to try him on a selective SSRI, Effexor. He didn't like the idea, said he had found amphetamines to be most helpful. I couldn't imagine anything worse."

"Did he say anything about Tegretol a primary care physician had apparently prescribed some time ago? He told me that was what he wanted you to renew."

"I asked him, and he denied mentioning it. Said he must have gotten the name wrong, or maybe you did. Funnily enough, Tegretol can help with mood swings in bipolar cases, but I doubt that's his disorder."

"How strange. I'm sure he said Tegretol. I feel I'm floundering, Ali. I was wondering about psychopathy."

"That's a good call. Can we get him to disclose any signs of an anti-social past? It's hard to make that diagnosis without a history. I couldn't get anything from him about his childhood, teenage years, or high school record. Could you pursue that a bit more?"

"I would normally, but Barbara has been leaning on me to back away from formal diagnostic issues and to establish a more trusting therapeutic relationship."

"Hmm," Ali sounded unimpressed. "Don't be too trusting. One thing I can tell you—maybe you know—he likes guns, owns a couple and has a license for a Glock handgun. Maybe he isn't a psychopath, but he sure reminds me of a lot of GIs I encountered in Iraq—the kind of young men who liked to mask their fear with brazen aggression, waving guns around and intimidating villagers. All swagger, with tattoos of sidewinders. Not all of them, but there were too many for my liking—Rambo types. Of course, they were real soldiers facing real dangers, not an immature student like Curtis, play-acting with what looks like a Celtic symbol on his neck—you must have seen it."

"Did you end up writing a prescription for him?"

"He was so insistent I prescribed a low dose of Xanax. Told him to take it three times a day, avoid alcohol, and to come back in three weeks and tell me how he's feeling. I don't think it could hurt, and it will help him sleep at night. He says he's restless and doesn't go to bed until the early hours of the morning. He's an odd bird, all right."

"I'm sure 'odd bird' isn't in the DSM-5, Ali!"

They both laughed, and then talked casually for a few more minutes, but after Ali left her office Katrina was unsettled. Just when she thought she had a new strategy and a plan for moving forward, the worst of her old fears were coming back. Why did Curtis have such low scores on Scale 4, Pd, of the MMPI? The Psychopathic Deviate scale should measure at the very least rebelliousness and lack of acceptance of authority—two traits that seemed to characterize him only too well. He said he'd answered the questions honestly. Yeah, right. There's always a logical conundrum when an inveterate liar says he's telling the truth.

The phone rang in her office. She picked it up. The screen said 'unknown number'. "Hello?" No answer. Beep. Someone had hung up. Katrina called the campus operator and asked if she could trace the call. The operator laughed out loud. "Not unless it was from overseas. Everything else is fully automated."

"Can I call it back?"

"No, if your screen read 'unknown caller' it means the caller is using some kind of blocking command. You said you're calling from the health center. Calls are all supposed to go through your receptionist; why did she put it through?"

"There's a direct number as well, in case we need to accept or make calls after hours. We don't give that number out to anyone."

"Well, someone got your number. Unless it was a robocall. We're getting a few; campaign season is starting. Sorry I can't help you."

Katrina asked the other intern, Dharia: "Are you getting any nuisance phone calls? I've had a few the last couple of weeks, on the internal line."

"No. Sorry. Why not keep a log of times and see if there's a pattern? Or set it to go direct to the answer system and only pick up if you recognize the number on the screen."

"Good ideas. Bye. See you tomorrow!"

When she got home, Tony Richardson, her landlord, came out his back door to chat.

"Been enjoying the backyard, Katrina?"

"What? Sure, Tony, it's looking great now that the spring green is everywhere, but I've not had time to go outside, to be honest."

"Really? I thought maybe you had been out having a stroll or two."

"Not I. When the summer is finally here, I'll drag one of your Adirondack chairs out back, if I may, and catch the sunshine."

"Of course, you're welcome to, but I thought you had already. I was out back the other day raking up some of the dead twigs and pine cones, and I noticed some footprints. The wild daffodils are mostly over this late in April, but some of them were trampled on. It didn't seem like it would have been you, but I thought I'd ask. I don't like the idea of people wandering back there. Some years ago, one of the neighbor kids discovered it was a quick way to get to that little creek at the end of the property where they sometimes played. I asked them not to and they stopped. They're good kids. But maybe they've got a new game."

"Well, it wasn't me. But I'll keep an eye out, and if I see them I'll tell them off—most politely, of course!"

Only when she got inside and had hung up her coat and sorted through the junk mail did it suddenly occur to her. If it wasn't the neighbor kids, who the heck was it? What would anyone need to go back there for? Although Tony acted like it was a real backyard, it was more of a wilderness—lots of times he didn't even bother to go out with the weed eater and clear some of the growth. Raking pine cones sounded like a first to her. Maybe he had seen his own footprints, just like Pooh Bear and Piglet walking in a circle in the snow and looking at their footprints and thinking they were being followed. That would be Tony. He was getting on in years. God, he must be over sixty now. Easily confused. All the same, that evening she turned off all the lights and sat in the big armchair looking out at the trees. She was uneasy, so she poured herself a glass of wine and sat sipping it for about half an hour before going to bed. There was enough moonlight. She thought she maybe saw a deer, but couldn't be sure. She certainly saw no kids, nor anyone else.

Chapter 13: Seek and Hide

Dr. Ali Abidi was not, generally speaking, a particularly reflective psychiatrist. His medical training at Yale had been hard science focused, and his own school background had emphasized the natural sciences. That was probably one reason he had found Miss Adilah Sharine of New Haven, Connecticut, so utterly charming. He'd never encountered a girl before to whom he could talk, without boring them, about some of the latest amazing advances in medical technology. And Yale's medical school curriculum was heavily evidence-based. "Don't rely on subjective clinical judgment," the professors insisted, "make sure you call for the appropriate lab tests. What you can hear through a stethoscope is but a fraction of the messages you receive from a stress EKG and an ultrasound and everything else in the modern doctors' digital bag." And when he went to Baghdad for the psychiatry residency, they were busy doing all they could to abandon any traditional indigenous medical practices and make sure they were up to date with making the right DSM diagnosis and prescribing the right, latest FDA-approved-in-America drug to treat it.

But a patient like Curtis Pierson was a bit of a challenge to the science of formal diagnosis. He met the criteria for any number of syndromes, and Miss Moss, whom people said was a good psychologist, had made no apparent progress with psychological tests. Mr. Pierson required a little more careful thought. Could he be a serious danger to the campus community? It was not at all clear to Ali. What sort of violence was he capable of? Predicting violence was difficult; past behavior was a good indicator, but no one seemed to know much about Curtis's past. He did not have a criminal record, as far as anyone knew.

There were, however, some oddities about his psycho-social history. Ali had done a cursory interview regarding his background, but Curtis had been evasive. Katrina hadn't learned much more, apparently. She had told him there was some mystery about Curtis's birth mother and for what reason he'd been adopted, his last name changed, and why he was not permitted any contact with the woman who had given him life, and who might herself no longer be alive.

There was one other piece of information Katrina had obtained, which she had rather quickly tried to dial back once she had mentioned it, saying she shouldn't have told anyone, even the psychiatrist with whom she was collaborating on the case—Curtis had made her promise not to. It was his middle name, which he didn't use and was not on any official records, even his driver's license, and certainly not on the university student record system. The secret name Katrina had leaked was Fairfax.

Ali googled 'Fairfax'. Not helpful: lots of stuff about Virginia, Mount Vernon, other points of historical interest, maps. He thought for a moment. *Where did Curtis say he was born? Maybe he didn't.* Ali wasn't into demographic details. *What had Katrina said? Something about northern Pennsylvania.* That was no help: there was no Fairfax in northern Pennsylvania, according to Google. 'Near

Binghamton' rang a bell. He looked at a map. The little town of Great Bend, unimaginatively named for a bend in the Susquehanna River, was near Binghamton. It was worth a try. Enter: 'Fairfax, Great Bend, PA'.

That was it. An old newspaper story, from twelve years ago. Jonas Fairfax, thirty-six, shot to death in his home with his own 12-gauge shotgun. Close range, right in the middle of his chest. It's possible he was seated in his armchair at the time. He had a drinking problem. His wife, Judi, was arrested and charged with second-degree murder. Their only son, name withheld, was home at the time. Jonas was known to be abusive. Sheriff Deputies had been called to the house on numerous occasions. Judi had sustained injuries. County child protection services had been considering removing the boy from the home after evidence of a severe beating, but a social worker's report argued that the boy and his father had a good relationship and went hunting together. The boy had a mentored youth hunting permit.

Why was that last item relevant, Ali wondered? He re-Googled 'Jonas Fairfax murder case, Great Bend', and found a couple more articles. It wasn't exactly the crime of the century, but it had caused a stir in Susquehanna County. The trial was straightforward. Judi had called 911 and said she had shot her husband. Only her fingerprints were on the shotgun. The abuse and violence in the household were considered extenuating circumstances, but there wasn't much leniency. Judi Bashira Fairfax got twenty years, and the boy was sent to a foster home, out of state. Details were sealed by order of the oddly named Clerk of Orphan's Court, in Montrose, PA. Ali stared at the mother's name with some interest. Curtis was indeed an enigma.

The other articles covered much the same information. There was a brief mention of only one inconsistency in an otherwise open and shut case. An eyewitness reported seeing Judi outside the local Burger King at about the time the coroner estimated the time of death, but fifteen minutes before the 911 call. She was known in the small local community, but Judi said the witness must have been mistaken, she had been home all afternoon. She always tried to be home when her son got out of school—she didn't approve of latchkey children. The coroner could easily have gotten the timing wrong. Jonas had been drinking—that would affect his metabolism.

Ali might have had a rigorous scientific training, but he had also seen a lot of horrible forensic cases in Iraq. The constant violence, bombing, shootings, and general mayhem masked a great deal of simple crime as well. Crimes of passion, like this one. But would a mother—yes, perhaps driven to desperation by a drunk abusive man, as her defense lawyer described it— assassinate her husband, at close range, while her son was home from school?

Ali thought it unlikely and had another scenario in mind. The boy had had one beating too many. He knew how to use a shotgun; maybe he just pointed it at his father to scare him off. Whatever. The son shot him, and when his mother came home she knew the consequences—sure he was a juvenile, but courts were getting tougher with youth, even ten-year-olds. The mother wiped the shotgun clean, handled it herself, called 911, confessed, and then made the boy change his clothes, wash his face and hands, and dump his clothes in the washing machine.

She was obviously guilty; there'd be no careful crime scene investigation. All the boy had to do was to stay cool and keep his mouth shut. His mother would reassure him everything was going to be okay—she had bruises, it was justified. But it was not okay. He never saw his mother again—she was a convicted killer and his identity needed to be protected. But it was he who was violent, and now his blood ran cold. His guilt had to be repressed. No loyalty, no compassion: only to a mother whom he could hardly remember any longer. She had taken a bullet for him. One day, he would honor that, and her, and her sacrifice.

Ali was not convinced of the accuracy of his version of the story and his psychological profile. Even so, he should tell Katrina of his suspicions, but she had just been asked to take a different perspective. As long as Curtis wasn't overtly violent or making direct threats, there was no immediate danger and no need to act precipitously. In a way, you almost had to admire a mother or a son who had the guts and the passion and their loyalty to each other to get their revenge on a physically abusive, worthless drunk like Jonas Fairfax appeared to be. Ali decided it would be better to wait for an incident or a tangible sign that there was a threat. In the meantime, he had his own problems. His depression, his anger and his self-loathing that was so acute after the death of Adilah, was returning. He knew the symptoms only too well.

Chapter 14: Suspicion

From Curtis's point of view, it was a bad evening. It was cold and it was raining, and after the burst of warm spring weather was over, Katrina Moss seemed ill-disposed to prance around her beautiful converted barn studio in the nude. Curtis watched her making dinner for herself wearing a long, loose sweater. Yes, she had taken off her jeans and replaced them with loose, flowery pajama bottoms. He'd seen a flash of her cute panties. It wasn't much, but still interesting, sort of like sharing her intimacy, getting to know her habits, and the thrill of expectation. He kept hoping she would decide to take a shower. The tension was high, but his discomfort was considerable. He was getting a cramp and the light rain was fogging his binoculars.

Suddenly, he saw Katrina plonk down on her sofa and pull her jeans back on again, then stand up and take a puffy down skiing jacket from her closet. Fuck. She was going out. Why? It was surely close to her bed time. It must be after nine o'clock. Is it possible she'd come around to the back? Had she seen or heard something? Fuck. He had to hide. He scrambled to get down off the branch he'd been half-sitting half standing on, but his foot slipped on a wet branch. He fell heavily the six feet or so to the ground, and grunted in pain. Fuck. His ankle was on fire. He must have twisted it. He crouched in some dense bushes, cursing. Then he realized if she was going out, she would have to drive past his car parked on the road—quite far down, but still obvious on such a lonely stretch. Fuck. He didn't hear her front door slam or her footsteps down the side lane, but he heard her start her car and drive off. Okay, that was something. If he could walk, he'd better get the hell out of there.

*****

Katrina wanted to make a cup of hot chocolate after her dinner. It was a rather miserable evening. Not cold enough to light the open fire that was at one end of the big studio, but chilly enough to need the old long sweater she'd had since her undergraduate days at Penn State. She opened the fridge. Damn. She was out of two percent milk; indeed, she was out of any percent milk, even the half-and-half she put in her coffee. She had raised her anticipations for a nice cup of hot chocolate. Was it worth going out to Wegmans, way over on the other side of Chenango Bridge? Nah, it was late. She sat down, resigned, and then suddenly thought maybe she needed some bread for toast tomorrow morning. Okay, that did it. She slipped off her pajama pants, reached for the jeans she had hung over the back of a chair when she got home, pulled them on, grabbed her jacket, picked up her keys, and headed for the stairs down to her front door.

Half-way down the stairs she thought she heard a thump. She stopped mid stair, and listened. Nothing. Probably a raccoon. They liked the garbage bins. Nevertheless, she put on the outside light above her front door and marched briskly down the path to her car.

She drove along Squirrel Hill Road for about quarter of a mile until she came to the junction where a right turn would take her across the bridge to the strip mall. Suddenly, she slowed down. There was a car parked on the side of the road. It was a black SUV. Curtis Pierson had a black SUV. She was going to back up to try to read the license plate, but a car was coming down the hill behind her and she had to move on. She didn't get any of the numbers or letters.

On her way back, she had her milk, her bread, a can of whipped cream, and a packet of marshmallows—if she was going to go to all this trouble to make hot chocolate, it might as well be the deluxe version. When she came to her corner, she slowed right down. The SUV was gone. Damn it. Curtis had a black SUV. As did thousands of other upstaters—the moms used them for getting kids to soccer and the dads found them useful for schlepping all their hunting gear around. Barbara had told her not to be paranoid. She was getting spooked—she had to stop it. It could have been anyone, and yet there weren't any houses on that end of her road.

*****

It was a couple of days later that Curtis Pierson hobbled into her office for his regular appointment.

"Goodness, Curtis, what have you done to yourself?" She sounded genuinely concerned and Curtis relished it. He winced theatrically.

"Sprained my ankle. Twisted it. I had to have it x-rayed. It's in a protective elastic support, but it hurts like hell."

"I'm sorry to hear that. How did it happen? Did you fall?"

"Yeah, I tripped and fell. I was running away from a mob of white supremacists that were chasing me."

Katrina didn't smile. She was getting tired of his bullshit. "Come on, be serious for once."

"But it's true. I guess I haven't told you, but for the last few months I've been attending meetings of this wacko group who meet in the old VFW hall behind the Fenton fire station—"

"Why in God's name would you do such a thing—are they the KKK? Surely you're not a member?"

"That's three challenging questions, Miss Nosey Moss. But for your information, I started attending because I was interested in what people were thinking about the ISIS threat. I'm curious about how crazy radical groups work. Like ISIS. It's fascinating. What do people think when they get radicalized? The press loves that word, but what the fuck does it mean? Turns out this group is just as crazy. They're like neo-Nazis or something. They don't wear hoods and burn crosses, but their attitudes and beliefs are the same. They're total racists and are open about it. They're anti-government. Right now, they are raising money to help in the legal defense of that psycho who was camping out on Federal land out west somewhere. The first meeting I went to, they were blaming the Jews for abortion, although it is their own ugly daughters who get knocked up and are desperate not to bring any more loser kids into the world—"

Katrina impatience was growing and she couldn't stop herself from interrupting.

"You can't expect me to believe all this?"

"It's true. I bumped into Dr. Abidi in the hallway and told him about it. He believed me. What I wanted to do was to see his reaction when I told him I was trying to understand the ISIS cult by exploring these radical groups. He didn't flick an eyelash, just stared at me, rather jadedly I thought. Great poker face, covers up anything. In any case, these idiots are not such a good example. We mostly get lectures from weird people, and the group can't decide what they believe. They're called STAND—Southern Tier Aryans for National Decency. I think they started as an anti-gay-marriage group in one of the fundamentalist church groups around here.

"Then we had a lecture on the sins of abortion from some retard from Harpursville, and then a discussion of whether we should join a new group called White Lives Matter More, and then they had an impassioned appeal from the chief of the campus police about CVSU academics blocking their right to bear rocket launchers or some shit. But somehow he recognized me and stopped in mid-dump, pointed at me, and said I was a student and shouldn't be there—and the bouncers came towards me. I ran. They chased me for a while and only gave up when I shouted to them I was an undercover FBI informer. But as I turned a corner, I twisted my ankle on some fucking pothole in the sidewalk."

"Curtis, I feel you are trying to impress me with tall stories. And it's a silly but serious accusation to claim Officer Gary Finch is out talking to right-wing extremist white-supremacy groups. He could lose his job, so be careful about who you're defaming. I'm on a committee with him, so I know he's a decent guy."

"Well, he's got you, the brilliant psychologist, fooled then. Dr. Abidi seemed very interested in what I told him. One of you should report the guy. Finch, huh? I didn't know his name; I just knew who he was. And somehow, he knew me."

"Can I ask you a different question? Were you parked on the road I live on a few nights ago?"

"I don't know where you live, Katrina."

"On Squirrel Hill Road, sort of out in the country, just past North Fenton."

"Oh, is that where you live? No, I don't remember parking there."

"Well, I saw your car on the side of the road."

"How do you know my car? Are you stalking me?" Curtis's smirk replaced his innocent look.

"Because when you come for your appointments, you always drive into the restricted staff-only parking lot and pull into one of the handicapped spaces. I've been meaning to have the receptionist call the campus parking guys and have you clamped."

"Well that's a bit hostile, isn't it? What about just a polite warning note on the windshield? I've sat in your waiting room so many fucking hours. I know you don't have any handicapped clients. And since you think I'm a serious mental case, I reckon I've got a serious disability—a mental handicap. There are lots of black cars around. How would you know it was me who parked on the squirrely hill?"

Katrina took a chance at a little fib. "I saw your license plate number; a black SUV."

For the first time Curtis looked uncomfortable. "What day was this?"

"It was quite late in the evening on Tuesday."

"Oh, Tuesday," he said with exaggerated expression of un-puzzlement. "Let me think. Hmm. I first went to the library at the end of the day, like I always do, and then went home and showered. I was visiting my girlfriend that evening. We're passionate; I'm hot for her. But it was the first time I was going to her house, and I got lost. I guess I stopped somewhere and texted her for directions. I didn't know I stopped on Chipmunk Lane—never heard of it before. I was way confused—she lives on the other side of the river."

"Squirrel, not chipmunk, I'm pretty sure the car was empty when I drove past, and there were no parking lights or headlights on," Katrina persisted.

Curtis shrugged. "If you know my car, you know I've got tinted windows. Anyway, I doubt it was my car you saw. Could've been, but there are lots of black SUV's around."

Katrina felt the old anxiety and feelings of distaste rise in her mouth like dry nausea. She hated the doubt almost as much as she hated the feeling that Curtis was not just stalking her but playing a devious game, one for which there was no specific point or advantage to be gained and therefore no rules. And he was sort of admitting that it was him, while in the same breath trying to deny it by obfuscation and uncertainty. If he would just admit it, he wouldn't be the first client to form an inappropriate interest in his therapist, and then they could deal with it in session. But if she outright accused him and was wrong, it would be damaging to the relationship. And according to Barbara, it was the relationship that was the therapy for now. She tried one more, quick probe. A sudden, unexpected question might just catch him out.

"What night did you sprain your ankle, Curtis?"

"That would be Wednesday. I got it x-rayed on Thursday. Today is Friday, our usual appointment time. If you're trying to trip me up, I'm afraid a big pot hole has already done that. Maybe this is a mental status exam, Katrina? It's 2015. This is a university clinic for nut cases. I can also name the current president, vice-president, and governor, but sorry, not the mayor of Fenton. I don't even know if there is one."

"All very funny, but now we're seriously wasting your time and mine. Can you try listening and focusing and let's get on with the session I had planned, talking about the times when you are feeling down. Not when you fell down."

Katrina tried to regain some lost ground with a little mildly sarcastic humor of her own. But she regretted it—it didn't sound warm, genuine, or empathetic, the key features of the client-centered approach her supervisor was encouraging. But how do you *act* genuine—that alone was an oxymoron—with someone who was so full of shit and could so easily put her on edge?

Chapter 15: The Security Committee

Roger MacDonald was beginning to feel overwhelmed as the latest meeting of the Security Committee got under way. Why, for God's sake, had he allowed Susan Kraus to coerce him to form and chair a committee like this, under the direct scrutiny of the campus president? It had an unlimited brief—way beyond the original issue of recommending a solution to the inevitable controversy about assault rifles for the campus police. After his meeting with the provost, a directive had come from her asking the committee to develop a set of contingency plans for campus emergencies, especially the presence of a shooter. She said most universities nowadays had such plans, and all the schools in the region had their drills. Roger hated the whole idea because it reminded him of the stupidity and paranoia of the duck and cover nuclear drills. But he had to admit that if there ever were an incident, and the campus had no plan of any kind, they would rightly be held accountable for how it all went down.

Tonya Evans had changed the dynamics of the group. As Roger suspected, she was one-hundred percent pro President Michaels. Now Phil Cohen was revealing himself to be supportive of some sort of new direction and allowing greater fire-power for the campus police. He kept saying that he saw the whole discussion in strategic terms—he saw it like the principle of mutual assured destruction that had kept the peace during the cold war. If the police were adequately equipped, no one would think of perpetrating violence on the campus—and the police would never have to use their new weaponry. Gary nodded enthusiastically. Marcia chimed in that the acronym for that doctrine, MAD, captured the true nature of that strategic principle. Katrina said she thought the students would feel less safe if the campus police went around with machine guns. Gary Finch said semi-automatic assault rifles were not machine guns.

Roger thought it might be a good idea to take a straw vote on whether to recommend Chief Gary Finch's request. He should have realized that was silly—the vote was three in favor, three against.

"Well, as Chair, I have a casting vote, but I don't want to use it. I think we should obtain something closer to a consensus which we can take back to President Michaels and that he can use in the event he gets criticism—as he is sure to, regardless of which way he goes. I do feel we need to talk some more about it. I'm wondering, since some of us don't know the difference between a semi-automatic gun and an automatic one, if Gary would present us, at the next meeting, with some specifications of the actual guns he is asking for. That would allow us to make a more informed recommendation."

Roger pushed his glasses back up on his nose with his index finger. Katrina, who had been watching him during these meetings, recognized it as a gesture of 'what the heck should we do now?' He was not exuding confidence, and she felt sorry for him. Drain Brain was a smart guy, but unworldly. She tried to help him out.

"Hey Roger, what a brilliant idea. Maybe Gary could get some reports from those campuses he says have already gone down this road, and could tell us what their experience has been. Don't need to run our own experiment if others have already tried it out. But what if we now, as a group, turned our attention to what lockdown procedures we'd like to introduce, and how to make students aware of them without scaring the bejeezus out of them.

"The campus is working on some good principles around sexual safety and consent, and they are being received well. Dave Gordon was working on these, and now Dr. Harriet Wilkinson in Psychology is leading the whole initiative. I think the time is right for the students to be more safety conscious as well. And I'd love some help with what we are doing at the counseling center.

"Remember I told President Michaels we were developing special instructions for faculty, or anyone, to report concerns or suspicions about any student acting erratically or talking about violence? And that we might be able to encourage them to come in so we could do some psychological assessment? Well, we're not nearly as far along as I'd like, talking frankly as a staff member. We're not even on the same page in the Center, as some of the counselors see this whole discussion as a massive invasion of privacy. I used to think that. But right now, I've got a client who worries me about his emotional stability and propensity for violence. We're keeping a close watch on him, and I can't say more; but my understanding is that if we thought he was becoming a danger to the campus community, it would be this committee that would authorize a formal response. That's why we need good procedures. It makes me feel a lot better that a concern could be brought to this group so the president—and Chief Finch here—could be given guidance regarding how to react.

"In the past, if we've had a client who seemed to pose a threat, we've contacted the campus police and left it to them, which is kind of unfair given they don't have any mental health training, do they Gary? Two years ago, when I was just a practicum student at the Center I had to ask campus security to come and pick up a student who was in my office, threatening suicide. I wouldn't let him out of the room and when the two officers arrived they took him off to the Emergency Room at Binghamton Hospital. Because as you know that's at least forty-five minutes' drive away, they asked me to come along in their squad car. I think all three of us were super anxious—all four, if you include the client, who didn't know what was happening and hadn't even given consent.

"That's why I know how crucial it is to have training, to have the campus police on our side, and I think if we agree on some simple common-sense procedures, then when there is a real threat, we'll all be a lot better off."

Roger smiled at her, nodding furiously. She was such a clever and sensible young woman and had a deft touch for handling potentially explosive committee conflict. Maybe you learn that in psychology—you certainly don't in hydro-engineering. If only he were younger and less dreary, he'd love to take her out, get to know her much better socially—as a friend, of course. She's not actually a student, is she? As an intern, surely she was a fellow employee? That wasn't against the rules, was it? If only he were twenty years younger. He mentally slapped himself on the hand. *Stop it! Stop even thinking such thoughts. Christ, you don't want to become one of those old campus sleazes who were still around on the faculty. You should be one hundred percent professional, the way she is.* But he did allow himself to admit that if it ever came to some sort of vote, he'd likely support any position she'd vote for. He was infatuated. Surely there was nothing wrong with that?

Getting the committee on task was the best antidote to Roger's wild thoughts, and he now focused on the design of drills. For the next couple of hours, the committee worked hard, and here Roger was effective. He was good on details and data. He had gathered together some lockdown procedures from other universities, easily available on the Internet. They were all obvious. The first thing they did do was declare themselves the Unified Incident Command Team. A designated text address for priority messages could get them assembled at lightning speed. They would be able to coordinate everything. Student and faculty procedures for a lockdown were approved. Simple—stay where you are, close windows and blinds, and lock or barricade doors. Mute cellphones and stay quiet. Never open the door until ordered to by a campus official with ID. Don't set off a fire alarm. TRY to stay calm. If you have friends or loved ones in Fenton, text them you are okay, but ask them to stay away; the roads need to be kept clear for emergency vehicles. There were a whole lot of other pieces of valuable advice. The procedures would be announced in the student newspaper, and faculty would need to undergo a brief training course and be certified they had done so. Marcia objected to this, but was overruled. Students would need to record their cell phone information centrally with the University Registrar so text alerts could be sent out. Marcia and Katrina both objected to this, saying it was unworkable, and maybe an intercom announcement would suffice, but they were overruled. Roger broke his recent vow and argued that some sort of system like this was needed, although he absolutely saw Katrina's—and Marcia's, of course—point of view.

Although he hated his role and the pressure it was putting him under, Roger adjourned the meeting feeling quite good. Everyone had little tasks to do to get everything into one cohesive document. The provost and the president were informed that the Security Committee was now the Unified Incident Command Team. It all felt it was going well. So well, in fact, it gave him confidence to do one more thing. He would ask Katrina out.

Roger wouldn't describe himself as lonely, exactly. But the idea of spending time getting to know Katrina had been constantly on his mind. He wasn't some old lech or perv, he reassured himself. He knew he was way too old, and, in any case, he wouldn't dream of ever coming on to her. But she was smart and attractive—gorgeous would be a better description. He thought about her all the time. It would be perfectly appropriate just to ask her to go to dinner with him one evening. He could get to know her better, watch her smile, and hear her stories about how she got to be a senior graduate student in clinical psychology. He knew he was a good listener. Women had always enjoyed his company in the past. But how to ask her without scaring her off or implying it was a date, or making her think it was anything other than a collegial interaction, a sort of extension of the lunch the six of them had had just a few weeks back?

At the end of this good planning meeting, Roger pulled Katrina aside.

"Can I have a word, Katrina?"

"Sure, any time. What's on your mind?"

Better just come out with it. "You are! I was just wondering, if you're not tied up one evening, if I could take you out for a meal. I'd like to get to know you better, and hear about your work. I'm not hitting on you, Katrina, at least I hope you don't think I am or find this awkward, I just think it would be nice. Totally casual. Maybe we could go to that restaurant which was converted from an old fire station—what's it called? Prometheus's Tavern. Silly name, because Prometheus gave us fire rather than extinguishing it, but that's Fenton for you. All they know about the Greeks is Spiro's diner on the Parkway. Sorry, I'm rambling. Hope I'm not freaking you out. I won't be offended if you say no or you're too busy or you're a vegan…"

Katrina wasn't uncomfortable, but surprised. She liked Roger and was impressed by his gentleness and sympathetic to how he seemed quite out of his depth trying to manage this strange committee. She felt, however, he needed some support and maybe this was his way of soliciting it. She was also just a tad flattered—it was nice to get the attention of a senior academic, much as she despised herself for thinking that, just as she despised herself for remembering she'd heard good things about the food at Prometheus's. She found shyness attractive in men and this seemed an entirely genuine effort at friendship, nothing more. And if she was wrong, she could handle Roger MacDonald without any difficulty.

She didn't necessarily have all those thoughts well-articulated in her mind, but they came together enough for her to say: "Yes, thanks, I'd like that. What date did you have in mind?"

"Oh, it wouldn't be a date," Roger stammered. He was flustered at her ready acceptance—he had assumed she'd say no immediately.

"I know. I'm sorry, I meant what *day* did you had in mind!" She was smiling, so Roger smiled too.

"How about this Friday? Around seven? If you tell me where you live I could come and pick you up—"

"Then it would be a date, wouldn't it? I live hell and gone in the country. It would be better if I met you at the restaurant—I know where it is—and then we can retain our independence." She was laughing again, and Roger squirmed inside. She hadn't rejected him, but she had set some logical boundaries, and she'd agreed to have dinner with him. What a great girl she was.

The evening was a great success, Roger assured himself later. He ordered a fine bottle of red wine, more than he would normally have spent and way more than Katrina could have afforded. They both had the steak. They both had crème brûlée for dessert. They joked that they had similar tastes and Katrina had a good appetite, which is always pleasing when you're treating someone to a decent meal. They both had coffee—Katrina had a decaf espresso and Roger had an Americano. Roger was conscious of a powerful feeling of attraction for her, but he showed it only by laughing at her jokes, asking lots of personal but not intimate questions, and paying close attention to her wants, like calling the waiter over to fill her glass with ice water and offering her a liqueur at the end of the meal.

Katrina enjoyed herself. Roger wasn't nearly as stiff or formal or even as dull as she had feared. He had only mentioned his cat Eugène once, in passing. Roger had been around and had some good stories—about his childhood in Illinois, and his time in New Zealand. He mentioned Paris, where Katrina wanted to visit. He hadn't mentioned his wife, and she didn't mention a boyfriend. It was just pleasing to have someone be attentive without any hint of physical payback. This was the sort of uncomplicated relationship that was rare in her experience. More like having dinner with her dad. She felt no physical attraction, and in this there was a stark contrast with Professor Roger MacDonald. Vicarious pleasure, however, was all he needed and he was delighted with how well the evening had gone. They had formed a little bond, intellectual, and collegial, and even personal. Katrina liked him; Roger was entranced with her. Far from getting her out of his head, he was now thinking about her even more.

Chapter 16: The Whiff of Grapeshot

What Roger did not know was that at the same moment the planning meeting ended and he was hitting on Katrina, President Michaels was busy complaining to Provost Kraus. As was typical of faculty committees, he grumbled, MacDonald's group was now developing a whole string of policies and names for themselves that were not in their original terms of reference and that any resolution of their main task, about assault rifles, seemed no further on. Susan Kraus tried to placate him by saying they were a reasonable group and given a little time they would prove to be helpful and constructive. Michaels listened to her stony faced—not flat out dismissive, but clearly communicating a deep sense of doubt.

When Susan left his office, he decided she was far too soft to be Provost. He needed a number two, a deputy, with a bit more gumption. Supporting faculty was the key attribute of her role, but sometimes she needed to be in charge as well. She had a huge amount of power over the faculty—why didn't she use it? Jesus, he said to himself, he respected democracy and faculty and student opinions as much as the next man, but not if they were going to be stupid about it. He had learned a long time ago that delaying or deferring decisions usually led to calamity. In his experience, a bad decision resolutely made was always better than not making one at all. And the indecision was leading to end-runs, which was exactly what Susan had promised him wouldn't happen if a faculty committee was given the task. Finch, the chief of campus security, had made an urgent appointment and was coming in to see him in just a few minutes.

"Oh, come on in Gary, sit down. Can I have Greta get you a cup of coffee?"

"No thanks, Mr. President, I don't want to take up too much of your precious time."

"For goodness sake, call me Jack—or Professor Michaels if you want—I'm not in the White House, you know. Yet!"

Gary Finch smiled politely at the weak attempt at humor. He had never interacted with Michaels one-on-one before, and didn't know exactly what to make of him. Gary and his fellow officers of the CVSU campus police had been delighted to learn a retired general would be taking the job of University President. The previous president, Sarah DeLorean, had made a big effort to reach out to the local community, but she was so predictably PC she was thought to be something of a flake. For a long time, she had resisted even side arms for the campus police until overridden by a directive from Albany. Gary had had no time for her at all. Surely a distinguished general would have some balls? But now he also seemed to be wavering on the semi-automatic rifle issue and had set up the ludicrous committee that mousy little MacDonald, with his pedantic ideas, was chairing. It was time for Gary to go straight to the top.

"Well, Gary, what can I do for you?"

"It's about my request for semi-automatics for my campus police officers," he began.

"Now as I told you in my e-mail of some days ago, I've set up a high-powered committee to look into the matter." Michaels suddenly stopped and shook his head in bewilderment, exactly like a prize fighter who has just had a left hook delivered straight to the temple. "Good God, man, you're *on* the committee. You know more about what is going on than I do. You need to be strategizing and convincing your group, not coming to me."

"The problem, Professor Michaels, is they are all on one side and they're all against me. You would surely understand, from your extensive military experience, that if we have a shooter on campus, we have a potentially deadly situation that would get more perilous by the minute if campus security isn't able to take the shooter out immediately. The members of the committee have never encountered a dangerous person or a mental case armed with his own semi-automatics, whether rifles or pistols. The committee doesn't seem to realize there are more and more Muslim students on campus, coming as supposed refugees, but of whom we know nothing about their backgrounds."

Michaels tensed. This was exactly the kind of conversation he didn't want to have. He'd had more than enough experience of troops in Iraq who trusted their weaponry more than caution, common sense, or the de-escalation of tension, and it had always gone badly. Instinctively, he knew he essentially despised someone like Gary Finch. Maybe that was too strong a word for his feelings, but he could sense the man was rigid, not very intelligent, and unable to think outside the square regarding safety on campus. Although in Iraq, where everyone assumed Jack was a tough guy, what no one knew was that when working with civilians and family members of possibly radical scientists working on chemical and other WMDs for the old regime, he always used guile rather than force. A combination of velvet glove and iron threat inevitably worked to win over frightened parents, spouses, brothers, sisters; and to help them understand that it was in the best interests of their loved ones to tell him what they could. That would not be disloyal. It was not betrayal. It would save their lives and ensure they could be protected by the US presence. He also used moles when he could, but not after—Christ, he couldn't think of that, not now. Not ever. He tried to reason with Gary.

"I can assure you of the few actual incidents in this country of shooters on college campuses, none have been Muslims or Islamic terrorists. And you're quite wrong about us not knowing much about the students we enroll from overseas. We do a thorough check on their backgrounds, their academic experiences, their motives for coming to study at CVSU. Hell, we even work with the State Department and the immigration service if necessary. Of course, no one can say for sure that there are not people like the 9/11 terrorists living in our midst, but the odds are extremely unlikely."

"Are you willing to face the consequences of the rare, 'unlikely' exception?"

"Are you willing to state categorically that issuing assault weapons to the campus police would prevent any attack from ever happening?"

"Course not, Professor," Gary paused for a moment. He felt he was losing the argument. It was necessary to try a new direction. "But let me tell you about another threat I'm aware of that might be much more serious. I'm not only concerned about mentally ill or radicalized students on campus. I'm also concerned about hot heads in the local population."

"What! Here in peaceful little Fenton?" Michaels was laughing openly.

"Oh, sir, you know nothing about some of the groups in the community. You don't know that when Albany decided to build a campus here back in the sixties, they took away some of the best duck and deer hunting areas in the county, maybe the whole State."

"Good God, Gary, that was fifty years ago. Surely the local hunters have found some other good spots by now!"

"You can scoff, Professor, but some of the people I know and who I'm thinking of used to hunt around here with their dads—right where we're sitting in fact. Yeah, they still resent it. And they resent the snobbery of the university, to be honest. This seems like a little center of privilege in a region that is facing tough times."

"But the university brings in millions of dollars in funding and the students support all the local businesses—we basically support the entire region and provide lots of non-academic jobs for people—like you," he added unwisely.

Gary bristled. "I'm just telling you, Professor Michaels, there are angry people out there in the community who don't see it that way at all. All one of them has to do is get laid off, or get sick from the science labs polluting the aquafer, or find his kid hasn't got the grades to become a student here. That's the kind of thing which can make a guy snap and do stupid things, and I'm telling you they're out there. And they've all got guns they hunt with. That's my warning—take it or leave it." Gary stood up to go. His face was flushed.

"Listen Gary, don't think I'm unsympathetic. I've got the budget addition you requested on my desk. I promise I'll give it careful thought. In the meantime, do your best to keep talking to the committee and see if you can come up with some sort of compromise. They're all reasonable people. Thanks again for coming in."

After Finch had left, Michaels sat pondering the whole matter. He hated indecision like this. During his graduate studies, one of the moments in military history he had always been bemused by was how Napoleon had risen to prominence by taking decisive action against a rabble of Royalist protestors. He had turned his light cannon on them as they marched down the street. Let's give them a "whiff of grapeshot," Napoleon had said at the time. Brilliant. Could Gary Finch be right about dangerous rabble in the outside community? Violence was no longer the province of the lunatic fringe—extremism was creeping into the political mainstream. The most recent horrible incidents of gun violence in the country were not carried out by seriously deranged lunatics, but by ordinary, pathetic people who enjoyed pro-Nazi sites on the Internet, tweeted hateful thoughts as though anyone were attending to them, and hung the Confederate flag on their bedroom walls. The banality of evil.

Did he want to be the failed university president who had overreacted to threats by arming the campus police and causing widespread student and faculty protests and sit-ins? Did he want to be the disastrous university president who had failed to recognize a clear and present community danger and not taken reasonable steps to prevent a catastrophe involving the lives of students? What a classic dilemma, and why wasn't the goddamned committee being proactive and helping him out here?

He called the Chief Financial Officer and asked him some questions after explaining that it was a confidential inquiry. His money man was hesitant. There was no slack in the budget for such a major investment. Other priorities on campus would have to be shelved until next year. Michaels listened politely and asked him just to think about it and get back to him if he could work out a discreet way. He added at the end of the conversation that he thought it high time the position of Chief Financial Officer should be elevated to that of a Vice-President.

Chapter 17: Consultation

Katrina had too many questions in her mind. She knew that being on the campus security committee was making her much more aware of the need to prepare for and to prevent threats to campus safety than she had ever been before. Dr. Abidi seemed to be on her side, but he was evasive, she thought, and not much help. Her supervisor, Dr. Kennedy had taken a different position. She wasn't into diagnostics, and she obviously felt Katrina was just another overly conscientious and anxious intern. She'd seen it before, lots of times. For her, clinical supervision was practically an extension of psychotherapy—the purpose was to allow the trainee to dig deep into her own areas of conflict and vulnerability and to resolve emotional stresses that might bias how a healing therapeutic relationship would serve to give the client insight and the opportunity for self-actualization.

Katrina didn't fancy this style of supervision although she recognized her resistance to it was feeding precisely into Barbara's view of her as an overly mechanical, research-focused clinician who followed formulae rather than instinct. But for Christ's sake, she had now bumped into Curtis at the mall. When it was obvious she had spotted him, he came over and said he was visiting his mom. She worked near there. Plausible, but too much of a coincidence. And then she thought she'd seen his car again, near the Prometheus Tavern the evening she had gone out with Roger. It was driving away as they came out, and the thought of it had spoiled the rest of her night.

Dammit, she truly was getting paranoid. She needed a second clinical opinion, and that was why she decided to call Dave Gordon, who had until recently been director of the clinical psychology training program, but was now retired. He had supervised Katrina in past practica and had taught her the standard CBT protocols. She found him experienced and open-minded. She wouldn't tell Barbara she needed to speak to Dave.

"Where do you want to meet?" Dave asked on the phone, pleased to be wanted to talk over a complex case.

"Somewhere private, would your house be okay?"

"Of course, you remember how to get here? But I presume this means Dr. Kennedy doesn't know you're doing this?"

"Yes, I'm afraid it is right off the record. I just need some suggestions to keep me grounded here."

Sitting in a big armchair in Dave's study, littered with papers and journals, with a cup of strong French Roast coffee in her hand, Katrina told Dave as much as she could about Curtis.

"I'm going to use his real first name, assuming all this is private."

Dave nodded. He listened attentively before launching into some questions.

"Okay, Kat, let's start with diagnosis. If you had to give him a label, what would it be?"

"Narcissistic Personality Disorder."

"Spot on! He seems to meet the criteria: arrogant, false sense of superiority, thinks he's special, is interpersonally exploitative. So now we talk treatment options—"

"Wait, Dave, doesn't he seem to you to be a psychopath? That's why I'm worried he might be dangerous. I know I said I wasn't certain, but truthfully, I'm sure he's stalking me."

"But not threatening you? Or at least you haven't mentioned anything about anti-social acts, or violence, or aggression."

"I know he has a fascination with guns."

"But so do half the residents of this county, so that's not a symptom. What about anti-social acts?"

"Oh, I'd say he's pretty damn anti-social. Breaks all sorts of rules. And he's got this creepy lack of feeling for others. I've done a practicum at the county prison and talked to lots of offenders, but no one quite like him. He controls his emotions well."

"But as you know people in prison are not necessarily psychopaths. They just commit crimes, often related to economic need, and are not smart enough to avoid being caught. So, let's be systematic about this. If you want to label him a psychopath, you need to do some formal assessment, the MMPI, or better yet, the Psychopathy Checklist-Revised—the PCL-R…"

"What's weird is that I did administer an MMPI and his level of psychopathy, indeed all syndromes, was well below clinical cut-off scores."

"Maybe he fudged it somehow. You say he's clever? What about the PCL-R?"

"I think I need much more background information from other informants and past records to go with that. I can't get that sort of information on him—or out of him."

"So, as far as you know he's never committed a violent act? If he had, I'd be much more concerned about your sense he's a threat to you or the campus community."

Dave was silent for a while, pondering the issues. Finally, he switched seamlessly to mentor and professor and guru mode.

"Look here, as you know 'psychopath' is one of the most misused diagnostic categories in all psychiatry. I blame Hollywood. They love to create characters like Hannibal Lector. And the news media, anytime there is a mass killing, the perpetrator is described as a psychopath. But many of those mass killers have a clear motive. It is not that they lack a conscience, it is that they have a different set of moral values— their anti-social behavior is easily directed towards new enemies.

"You may know the most recent analysis of the psychopathic personality suggests there are three, maybe four main types. It is not just one homogenous cluster. I find the three-type analysis most compelling." By now Dave Gordon was in full lecture-theater mode, but Katrina was nevertheless in awe of his ability to have this range of information at his fingertips. "The categories are being manipulative, aggressive, or sociopathic. Sociopathic offenders are often hard-core criminals, but they have the capacity for guilt and remorse, which strangely enough makes them easier to treat. Curtis isn't in that group. The aggressive type describes people who use violence to get their own way and solve problems. That doesn't sound like Curtis either. But the third type, manipulative, also show low fearfulness, high social dominance, fetishism, deviant sexual behavior, but lower on anti-social traits—"

"Before you tell me that is the subtype which sounds like Curtis, I've got to ask how you remember all this stuff. You're retired."

"Retired, not brain dead. But I have a terrible memory, and the only reason I'm up on the research is that I recently wrote a little article on the topic. It got published last week—I'll e-mail the PDF to you."

"That sounds like a particularly good example of a humble brag to me."

"Gosh, Katrina, you become an intern and lose all respect for your elders and mentors. But while we're sitting here giggling at our own clever banter, what does this say about your patient? I'd say that 'psychopath, manipulative subtype' is a better diagnosis than narcissism, remembering that psychopaths also have an inflated sense of their own worth. But more concerning is their primary characteristic is a callous disregard for others, and that makes them dangerous.

"I hate to interfere with your clinical supervisor, but between you and me, I think Barbara is wrong about this case. I think he is potentially dangerous, and you need to keep assessing him actuarially and find out more about who he has a grudge against, who is thwarting the achievement of his goals, and what sort of hostility he shows to fellow students, or faculty, or the campus generally. You need to listen for threats and take them seriously. It's hard to predict violence, sure, but it doesn't just come out of the blue—there are always triggers, hostile ruminations, and chronic anger.

"If you look back at the cases of mass shooters that have been prominent recently, there were always signs. Their mental health professional always admits there was something, some little warning light; they just failed to take it seriously enough to act on it. Your job is to attend to and interpret the signs. But the one thing I feel reasonably confident about is that he is unlikely to be violent towards you, judging from the things you have told me about his interactions."

Katrina left the retired professor's house feeling about as confused as when she'd walked in. It was a plus that Dave thought Curtis would not harm her, but he was not at all reassuring that Curtis was not a danger to others. As she was his primary therapist, it seemed very unfair that the responsibility for monitoring any change in threat level was on the shoulders of a mere intern. Dave had not convinced her that Curtis wasn't homicidal, quite the opposite. Shifting the likely diagnosis from Narcissistic Personality Disorder to Psychopath, Manipulative Type just added to her confusion. Four years ago, in one of her first classes on assessment and diagnosis, the same damn Dave Gordon had gone on and on about the unreliability of psychiatric labels and in any case how useless it was to label clients as opposed to developing a good case formulation of their unique collection of assets and deficits. And now, with a real case, trying to make predictions about future behavior, not to mention trying to come up with a treatment plan that would help the young man, they were back to playing pin the tail on the DSM-5 donkey. Fuck it.

Back in the office, however, Katrina pulled herself together. Of course the case formulation approach was the way to go. It was exactly what she'd been trained to do. She sat at her laptop, creating a concise, clear picture of Curtis Pierson. Just use psychological principles, not insults—how had early experiences shaped his personality, what were his family relationships like, what good coping skills did he have, what were his vulnerabilities, who were his friends? The more she worked on this profile, her conceptualization, the more she realized she hadn't been able to obtain many answers to those questions. His private life was still a mystery to her, largely because he managed to avoid any self-revelation by clever, manipulative, tactics during their sessions.

One fact was clear. Curtis liked her, or he wouldn't keep coming back, he wouldn't be trying to impress her all the time, and he wouldn't try to play games with her. You could call the games manipulative, but in an odd way they weren't that different from the way boys in college had interacted with her on dates, back in her undergrad days. Some young men don't know how to get close to a woman, or how to be intimate without thinking they must show off. If he wanted to connect with her emotionally, surely it was a good sign, especially if he was a psychopath, lacking empathy. And that desire could be the way into a positive therapeutic relationship—it just took time. Maybe Barbara Kennedy had the right approach after all. Katrina relaxed. She had to stop being fearful. Curtis was the wounded mind, for whatever mysterious reason. Don't be fearful, but be vigilant. They are not the same things. Monitor signs, Dave had said; be objective. Good. She was back to being a scientist, not a victim; a hunter, not the quarry. Time to go back to enjoying her role as therapist. After all, Curtis had some positive attributes—at the very least, he was interesting.

Chapter 18: Dr. Abidi
Goes to Vermont

It was Friday, and Dr. Abidi had already seen a slew of patients. Psychiatry in this university setting was largely a matter or prescribing medicines, minor stuff, not the powerful psychotropics that could affect mood and emotion and thought processes. Even so, he was careful, and prided himself on not over-prescribing. He always asked questions of the patients— ninety-five percent of them of course being young students— about what other medications they were taking, including things students were often into, like omega-3 fish oil, or the latest fad in high potency vitamins that might interact dangerously with the FDA-approved list of meds at his disposal. And his patients being mostly students, he also had to ask about alcohol abuse, and marijuana use, even contraceptive pills. Americans were being over-medicated; every good doctor knew that.

Ali Abidi also admitted he was very depressed. Maybe not yet at a clinical level, although he had in the past experienced severe and incapacitating bouts of major depression. Right now, he was deeply sad. He was still grieving. His wife Adilah Sharine had been killed in Iraq. Murdered, to be precise, and the thought of it, and her suffering, haunted him. How could he deal with this? He felt trapped, paralyzed. Adilah meant justice in Arabic, but it was ironic now—she had received none. Her middle name, Jewel, was derived from the French for joy, yet all joy had been taken from her and from Ali.

Adilah had been born in Damascus in 1971, the same year that Hafez al-Assad became President of Syria and started his one-man rule. She was the Sharines' ninth child, and as the last daughter born to aging parents, she was spoiled. Her parents were well-off and indulged her, but she was also the brightest of their children, and they dreamt of sending her to Paris for her university education. Her father, a successful diplomat, came from an Alawite family that had strongly supported the French mandate. The family spoke fluent French, but Adilah, who was good with languages, spoke excellent English as well. She was as good with languages as she was beautiful.

Although the Alawites were somewhat distrusted for having supported the French before they finally left Syria in the forties, Assad gave them authority over security and intelligence operations as well as the military. For a while, the Sharine family exercised and enjoyed considerable power. Yet it was a situation of constant danger, negotiating the endless sectarian conflicts Assad himself created in order to divide and rule. Not to mention the risks from his unpredictable personality and thirst for establishing a dynasty. It was decided that instead of going to the Sorbonne, Adilah should be sent to study in America. She excelled in science and enrolled in a Bachelor of Science program at Yale University, majoring in Biochemistry. In her junior year, she met a charming medical student from Iraq, named Ali. Ali adored her—she was beautiful, cultured, intelligent and thoroughly disrespectful of all religion, especially Islam and its hypocrisy. She was a modern woman. They got married in 1993, despite a distinct lack of enthusiasm from both of their families.

Ali wanted to go back to Iraq. He was offered a residency in psychiatry at the University of Baghdad—with an American M.D. and a biochemist for a wife, he was treated like royalty, but it was the worst possible time to return to a homeland he had left at the age of eighteen. Ali thought that having a presidential election meant some degree of democracy was returning to Iraq, but it proved to be a dangerously naïve hope. Saddam Hussein won 99.99 percent of the vote. It was obviously rigged; American sanctions had resulted in widespread shortages—voters were offered food.

Ali and Adilah developed a survival plan. They would not have children until they found a way to return to the US. Adilah's father had died, but she managed to bring her mother, now in her seventies, to Baghdad to live with them. Adilah took a job with a government-sponsored research lab, working on ways of detecting minute traces of explosives. Unfortunately, it meant she was working just outside Baghdad in a secret location. Ali finished his training and was specializing in adolescent psychiatry in a hospital in Baghdad when the American invasion began. It didn't take long. When the 1st Marine Division took over the hospital, Ali sought asylum. With his American English and Yale medical degree, he was instantly adopted and provided protection.

In the chaos of shock and awe, however, Adilah disappeared. Distraught, Ali did everything in his power to find her in the shattered city. No one knew anything or was willing to talk. There was a rumor that Adilah had been arrested by the Americans and taken in for interrogation. He pleaded daily with

American officials, yet there was still no information. But Ali was sure they were covering something up. 'National security' was the phrase they often trotted out. However much they liked him, he was still an Iraqi citizen. Trust took time. Months passed, and Ali became more and more desperate. The army medical officer serving as Ali's supervisor, Major Grant, M.D., promised to find out as much as possible and do all he could to trace her, but channels of communication were limited, Ali had to understand that. If she was in fact being held for interrogation, the major was confident she'd be back home soon.

She was. Adilah's battered body was dumped in the street outside their house in the early hours of the morning when Ali was on duty in the hospital. Her mother saw it and heard the screeching tires of a Humvee racing away, and she ran outside, screaming. Adilah was barely alive, and as she cradled her daughter's head, her mother desperately tried speaking to her in Arabic, French, and what little English she had. She later told Ali as much as she could about what Adilah had whispered:

"Tell Ali. Tell him. Tell Jacques."

"Who did this to you?" her mother asked, desperately.

"Jacques…please."

"Who's Jacques? Did he do this? What must I tell Ali?"

"Tell, tell him…kernel, kernel"

"Amande?"

"Non, ker…, k…Sand…Sanders, avec la canne."

"Jacques Sanders, did he do this?"

This time there was no answer. Adilah was already dead.

Ali questioned his mother-in-law over and over again to see if she could remember anything else. He felt he was going mad, but had enough composure to take the matter to US military higher-ups, demanding an enquiry. Major Grant backed him. There was indisputable evidence that Adilah had been tortured. He was told repeatedly they had no record of a Jacques Sanders working in any capacity, even for the CIA or for one of the nefarious private contractors that were involved in security and interrogations.

Everyone expressed sympathy, assuring him all steps were being taken to investigate this senseless killing, an apparent cold-blooded murder. It was much more likely to be insurgents than US military personnel, but inquiries were being made. If it were true she had been in US custody, the intelligence community's secrecy would be understandable. They had to be secretive. They had to be. Surely Dr. Abidi would understand? National security was at stake. The only comfort they could offer Ali was that if anything was ever discovered, he'd be the first to know. And if it proved to be the case that someone from the US armed forces had been involved, that person would face a court martial, their career would be over, they would be kaput, dishonorably discharged. Jacques Sanders, if he were ever found, would be finished, and ruined. The US did not sanction torture.

A high-ranking official from the State Department, who had set up an office in one of Saddam's former palaces, made Ali the final promise.

"Now look here Doctor Abidi, you have worked so well with us and been so invaluable, what we can do is offer you arrangements to be repatriated to the United States. We can get you a green card without a lot of bureaucratic paperwork, and we can help you find employment as a psychiatrist—

somewhere gentle and safe and accepting. Maybe a university clinic, somewhere in the northeast, maybe New Haven where you trained, or Amherst, or near Syracuse."

One year later, in the summer of 2008, Dr. Ali Abidi started working at the Chenango Valley State University student health clinic as chief medical officer and coordinator of mental health services.

Ali got up and fetched a cup of coffee for himself. It was all history now. He didn't even have a decent picture of Adilah, and the best one he had, he kept hidden in his desk drawer. Her lovely smile and gentle face contrasted too harshly with the traumatic memory of her disfigured body. He had to stop ruminating. Eight years was long enough to find some degree of acceptance. But the ghosts were returning, with a vengeance. He had to get away.

He looked at his weekly schedule on his smartphone and knew it was time for him to do some planning. Two days over the weekend should be enough time in Vermont, but he didn't want to rush back on the Monday, and that was a day he had scheduled Curtis Pierson for another appointment, along with a few other patients. Those patients could easily be rescheduled, but he wasn't so sure about Curtis. He was a time bomb, Ali thought, which was fine, but needed careful handling. He was especially keen to monitor his meds. It wouldn't be helpful if they were having such a strong sedative effect that he didn't want to go to his classes or come onto campus at all. Keeping a patient's routines normalized was important. But for the appointment, maybe Curtis would be willing to change to Tuesday—Ali had an opening at five. He thought it best to call

Curtis himself rather than have the receptionist do it. His reactions might be informative. He reached him right away.

"Oh, hello, Mr. Pierson, this is Doctor Abidi here. Yes, I'm fine thank you, how are you? Good, good. The reason I'm calling is I want to reschedule our Monday appointment. I've got to go away over the weekend and I won't be back on Monday. How about the next day, Tuesday, at five?"

"No can do, Doc. I've got a majorly important commitment on Tuesday at five. I have it every Tuesday at five. Regular as clockwork. You know me, Mister Fixed Habits."

Ali recognized the sarcasm. Both knew Curtis was one of the most erratic, unpredictable people you would ever be likely to encounter. But Curtis wasn't finished. It amused him to think he was dissing the important doctor for a trivial reason and he decided to rub it in. What a joke.

"You see Doctor Abidi," Curtis switched to a serious and solemn tone, "I have to be at the library *exactly* at five. It's the same every Tuesday. That is when the library staff offers free coffee and doughnuts to students, to encourage them to come in and use the library resources instead of sitting at home on their silly computers. And I must get there exactly at five or all the crullers will be gone, and I'll have to have a Boston cream instead, not nearly as good. It's my ritual, you might say, and a lot of students gather in the library foyer at that time—they go straight for my crullers."

Ali knew he was being played with again. Curtis was way too smart to be yakking on about doughnuts. But it was interesting information, nonetheless. Everything Curtis said, either straight or tongue in cheek, helped with the task of analyzing his rather twisted mind.

"All right, Mr. Pierson, that's okay. I could probably fit you between some other appointments on Wednesday morning, if you don't mind waiting a little bit."

"What else is new, Doc? I'm always sitting there waiting patiently to be seen, never complaining."

"Fine, let's say about 10. And you may get lucky, I may have a cancelation."

"Done," said Curtis and hung up.

Curtis sat in the sun on one of the wooden benches surrounding the smallest of the university courtyards, named after a famous furniture company which had started in the Southern Tier. It was a pretty spot because in the distance you had a view of Chenango Lake, where the willows were turning a bright green in anticipation of an early summer. He shoved his phone back in his pocket, and closed his eyes, thinking about the doctor. What could he be up to that he suddenly had to go away for a long weekend? Did he have a girlfriend? Curtis knew him to be single, a widower according to the gossip. If he was with ISIS, think how easily he could travel, without suspicion, to some other part of the country, and meet up with fellow terrorists and plot mayhem. Who would ever suspect a nice doctor, even if he was an Arab who had come from Iraq and who pretended to be non-religious? He would be under the radar of the NSA or the FBI. It would be easy to be more careful than that idiot Hasan, who was blabbing all the time about how unfair the US was towards Muslims. Only a nitwit would make a mistake like that.

Abidi seemed to be a pacifist, but that's a good cover. Curtis had noticed just an unusual flicker of interest cross Abidi's face when he told him he owned a Glock pistol. Curtis was a good observer of emotion, honed as a young child by needing to judge the mood his father was in. He thought Abidi sat a little more upright in his chair and asked him what model. That was a strange question. Curtis had answered, adding: "Do you know guns, Dr. Abidi?"

"No, no. I hate guns. I saw too much violence in Iraq."

Curtis regretted telling him about the Glock. It had been partially designed to shock him, as it did most people when he dropped the fact into a casual conversation. But Abidi had not been shocked, he had been interested. Fuck. That was a mistake. He wondered if he'd told Katrina. He didn't know how much they compared notes. Probably not much; psychiatrists had a low opinion of psychologists because they weren't real doctors. But maybe they talked about him because he was so interesting. However, Katrina had never mentioned it or asked him about it, despite always sneakily trying to probe for any tendency towards violence. She wasn't too subtle about it. Extremely cute, but no match for him in sensitivity—or in strategy.

Curtis should have been in class; there was a Friday afternoon tutorial for an economic history class he'd somehow been persuaded to take by some dumbass advisor at the beginning of the year, but fuck that. The sun felt good and he was in a satisfied mood. His thoughts about Abidi hadn't gone anywhere, but he knew one thing. The doc was going to be out of town for three days. With no possibility of being interrupted, this would be a good time to get into his office and try to find out exactly what sort of notes the doctor had on him and whether there were any telltale messages from some radical imam somewhere, one of those loonies dressed in nightgowns.

Sure, their outfits were no weirder than those of the Catholic priests, but since we couldn't understand the imam's language or know what they're preaching, it didn't seem unreasonable they should be kept under some sort of surveillance. This was one of the few things Curtis agreed about with the asshole members of STAND.

There were two big problems about breaking into the clinic over the weekend. One was that the clinic had a security alarm controlled with a keypad, and of course he didn't know the code. The other was that the front door, made of reinforced glass, was substantial and had a fucking great lock. He might be able to get through a window, but broken glass would reveal a break in. Then he remembered the men's toilet had a small hinged window above the two piss troughs. That might work.

On Saturday morning, Curtis showed up at the counseling center. It was closed, but Curtis knew they ran a gender identity workshop for students having conflicts over sexuality, homosexuality, cross-dressing, and the like. Saturday was a good day—none of the participants were keen to be seen there. He banged on the door, and eventually one of the female social workers came and opened it.

"I've come to see Dr. Abidi. I have an appointment," Curtis said.

"Oh dear, I think you've made a mistake. We never make individual appointments on a Saturday. Anyway, he's away for the weekend. When was your appointment?"

"Eleven o'clock on the 24th."

"Well that explains it! Today is the 25th! I've seen you here before. What's your name?"

"Daniel Defoe. That's Defoe with an 'e'."

"Okay, Daniel, call or come in again on Monday, and Debbie, the receptionist, will sort it out. Are you okay? You're all right for getting through the weekend? You know there is an emergency number…"

"Thanks, but I'm good. But I could use the bathroom, if that would be okay."

"Of course, that's just fine—you probably know where it is, down the hallway."

She had no hesitation at all. He was such a well-spoken, respectful young man, and like so many of the undergrads here, not knowing the day of the week!

Curtis sauntered down the hallway and into the men's room. It was deserted. All the participants in the group were women. He unlatched the window above the urinals, pushed it open a crack, and placed a large piece of chewing gum such that the latch could no longer engage. He then pulled the window closed. It looked shut, from both the outside and the inside. Curtis washed his hands noisily and came back to the front where the social worker was waiting to show him out.

"Thank you so much," Curtis gushed, and she smiled at him.

"Have a nice day!"

That afternoon Curtis moseyed down to the Fenton Salvation Army thrift shop and bought some clothes: brown loafers with a tassel, right out of the eighties, tan slacks, a plaid seersucker short-sleeved button-down shirt, and a linen jacket. It cost him twenty dollars. At about six-thirty, dressed to impress in this outfit, he drove to campus, parked, and walked about ten minutes across the mall to the health center. He made his way round to the back, jumped up to cling to the rim of the men's bathroom window with one hand and used a screwdriver to pry it open. He'd never done anything like this before, and his heart was beating fast. It was exciting. If he had time, he'd go over to Katrina's apartment later and check out the action there.

It was a gymnastic feat to pull himself up to the window and twist his body around to get inside. Good thing he was fit and strong and skinny. As he was coming down the other side, his hand touched the urinal. Shit, that's disgusting. He was in a hurry, but he just had to wash his hands quickly. He then ran down the hallway and turned on all the lights in the reception area. A warning signal was beeping and a red light on the touch pad was blinking—the alarm had been activated, and a legitimate person had thirty seconds to punch in the code. He quickly checked all the office doors. Great. One was open. It would do. Dr. W. Denny was the name on the sign. He searched the desk for one of the clinic appointment cards—it had 'Bill Denny, Psy.D.' printed on it. He stuffed one or two cards into his pocket and ran back to reception. There was a board which had photos of all the counselors and staff of the center that semester. He looked at Dr. Denny's photo and muttered to himself: *You ugly old bald shithead, you're getting a makeover.* Then he slapped on top of the photo a copy of his passport picture, already prepared with a little Blu-Tack. He unlocked the front door from the inside. The alarm screeched.

Curtis grabbed the phone on the reception desk and called the campus security office.

"Good evening, this is Bill Denny at the health center. I came in to collect some reports, and I seem to have triggered the alarm. I entered the code but I must have gotten it wrong.

145

Can you send someone over immediately to turn it off? Thanks guys, I appreciate it."

About four minutes later a young man arrived, looking about the same age as Curtis. He didn't seem like the regular campus police, just the night security fellow who helped students who'd locked themselves out of their cars, or rescued absentminded professors who'd lost their keys. He had a white shirt with the CVSU insignia on the sleeve, dark blue shorts, and a walkie-talkie tucked in his belt. Curtis thought he looked ridiculous.

"Very sorry to trouble you officer, I punched in the code, 6489, nothing happened so I thought I must have reversed the numbers and I re-entered 4698, but nothing happened then either, which is why I called you."

"That's not the correct code for this building sir, it's 5432."

"For real?" Curtis's surprise was genuine, thinking the counseling staff must be so stupid they had to be given an easy code to remember. "Has it just been changed?"

"I don't think so," the guard said, punching in the numbers, and the screeching alarm stopped suddenly. "There you go. You're working late. You should go home."

"I've got a few more cases to review and then I will."

"Just to prove I know my job, can you show me your ID?"

"Sure, absolutely," Curtis said, reaching for his back pocket. "Oh, shit." A look of horror on his face. "I changed pants this afternoon and must have forgotten to transfer my wallet. Oh dear, what now?" He patted a couple of pockets of his jacket, and then said with a note of triumph: "Hey, I've got my business card here," and handed Bill Denny's card to the guard. The guard looked at it and then surreptitiously glanced over at the staff picture board.

Satisfied, the guard said, "Well doctor, when you leave, be sure to re-arm the alarm; I'll check back in about half an hour."

"Thanks officer; oh, and you lock the door as you leave, that'll remind me in case I forget."

"Good idea, sir." The security guard must have had about the same low opinion of academic staff ability as Curtis did.

As soon as he was gone, Curtis went to work on Dr. Ali Abidi's office door. The internal locks had not been designed for great security, and using an old credit card he'd brought along—the oldest trick in the book—Curtis was soon inside. He pulled down the blinds and turned on the light and started looking for—well, he didn't quite know what, files maybe, notes, correspondence, especially anything about one Curtis Pierson.

On Ali's desk was a Google map of Vermont and a printout from the Internet showing things going on in Burlington. Okay, that's where he was off to. Curtis glanced at the list. At Club Metronome this Saturday it was half price burger night; Tribal Seeds were playing at Memorial Auditorium; there was a gun show at Battery Park; Bubble Magic at ECHO Lake Aquarium and Science Center; a workshop on Rural Emergency Medical Services at the university. Jesus, thought Curtis, even more of a backwater than Fenton. The Islamic Center of Burlington was offering a talk by someone from Canada, including dinner, but no ad for a gathering of ISIS recruits. Also, sadly, no files marked 'Curtis Pierson'. He turned the computer on, but of course it required a password. No way could he guess that, and he had zero hacking skills, so he turned it off again.

The center drawer of Ali's gray standard-issue university metal desk was locked. That made Curtis curious. He reached underneath and felt for the pins in the drawer that engage holes in the desk when the key is inserted and turned. Curtis used his screwdriver to retract them. They were spring loaded, so when one side was pushed in he held it back by inserting his trusty credit card. Then he did the other side, and, with a sharp tug, the drawer opened.

It didn't look like there was going to be much: a couple of samples from drug companies still in their blister packs, some paper napkins from the student cafeteria, a few pens and a loose assortment of memory sticks. His electric bill from NYSEG partially obscured a postcard from someone in Turkey, probably a secret message from the Peshmerga—oh no, they were fighting ISIS, not helping them. But right at the back, and hidden under this clutter, was a small folder held together with a ribbon. Curtis opened it. Some letters in Arabic script; that was no fucking help. Another old letter, this one from the US Army. Something about someone called Adilah Sharine—Curtis guessed it was a woman but he couldn't be sure. There were other official-looking letters and documents, but they were all in Arabic. There was a small pad on which Ali had been scribbling some notes. Curtis stared at it in absolute fascination. The date 'May 4th' was circled several times. There was the word 'Council' and then 'GPB'. The rest seemed just like scribbles. Amazing, but what was the significance of 'KFC'? Was he planning his lunch? Was he on Twitter? In the digital world it meant 'Keep Fingers Crossed'.

Curtis tried putting everything back exactly as he found it. He wanted to be out promptly—the promised half hour would soon be up. He went back into the reception room, turned off all the lights, and rattled the door to make sure it was locked. Then back to the men's room where he first pissed all over the floor, he wasn't sure why—some sort of primitive scent marking, but it made him smile. The evening was not a complete waste of time and was exciting, but it was too late now to go over to Katrina's place. He climbed out the window and dropped silently to the ground, remembering not to land on his bad ankle. He reached up, pulled away as much of the wad of chewing gum as he could, and pushed the window closed hard. He heard it latch. He walked slowly back to his car, keeping out of the campus street lights and feeling pleased with himself. He thought of the movie *Flawless*. Maybe this was going to be his new thing.

Chapter 19: A Tangible Threat at Last

It was Monday lunch time, and Katrina had a break, between bites of fruit salad and vanilla yoghurt, to check her e-mail. Nothing much, but one looked strange. She stared at the e-mail address: glock&spielen@yahoo.mail. She didn't recognize it. It was probably one of the many advertising sites filling her in-box and her junk mail folder all too frequently. The message line was odd: URGENT. The message itself was simple: 'attachment, with love'. She nearly forwarded it unopened to the University's IT service, which was well-equipped to deal with spam. But curiosity got the better of her and she opened the attachment. It was in the form of a poem. She read it with mounting apprehension.

Comfort not my twisted soul,
Useless your quest to douse the flame.
Rational reason, executive control,
Thoughts automatic, affect of shame,
Implicit schemata: spewed therapy jargon.
So many tricks up your devious sleeve
Few of them give me a mental hard-on.
Psychobabble's hopeless for rage to relieve.
Intricate games, but I'm well defended.

Expect no cure, oh doctor mine-
Rebel's cracked mind will never be mended.
Shooting to kill is the proof, is the sign.
Outrage by public is so soon forgotten.
No cause discerned? The boy was just rotten.

Katrina hit PRINT, ran from her office past the big printer located securely at the back of the reception office, grabbed the page, and barged into Barbara's sunny corner office. Fortunately she was free, just working on some reports.

"Oh my God, Kat, you look white as a sheet. What's wrong? Sit down. You're shaking. Whatever it is we can fix it."

"Look at this." She thrust the page into Barbara's hands. Barbara read it slowly.

"Is this from a client?"

"I presume so. I've never seen the name on the e-mail before."

"It came by e-mail? We'll be able to trace it."

"First tell me what you make of it."

"Well," she said slowly, her brow furrowed, "'relieve' is misspelled, if that's the word intended. If we take the discourse literally, it is someone telling you that therapy is of no value to him or her. Some of these words are direct from CBT, aren't they? 'Schemata', 'automatic thoughts'. From Aaron Beck's work, right?"

"In a garbled sort of way. It seems to me contrived. It's fourteen lines, like a sonnet, and the lines rhyme. It has a sort of pseudo Shakespearian texture to it. It doesn't feel to me like a genuine outpouring of emotion, but there is a strong theme of threat. 'Shooting to kill' is the indicator that the writer's mind is 'twisted' and broken and will not be 'mended' by therapy."

"Whoa, I think you're reading way too much into it."

"Christ, Barbara, what else could it mean? I think we should inform campus security right away. I think it's a threat."

Barbara sighed. This was further indication of Katrina overreacting. If you're training to be a psychotherapist, you should expect clients to be more than a bit weird—they're mentally ill by definition. Breaching a client's confidentiality is a grave business, and it could be any one of the clinic's patients, or just a prank of some kind. *Katrina's going to have to toughen up,* Barbara thought, *and we'll need to work on this more in supervision.* She tried a compromise.

"Tell you what. Let's call a quick emergency staff meeting as soon as we can get the senior clinicians together, show them the e-mail, ask them if they have ever had any communications from this address and ask them what they collectively think. I think that would be the responsible and *calm* response." She put a little unnecessary emphasis on the word 'calm'.

At four-thirty that afternoon there were no clients scheduled, and a group of four clinicians and the other intern gathered in Barbara's office with puzzled looks. What did she want that was so urgent? Barbara passed out copies of the e-mail attachment and let people read and digest it. There were murmurs and soft whistles through teeth. Dharia Williams, Katrina's fellow trainee, spoke first.

"Crap, Katrina, this sucks. You must know who it's from."

"No, not really, but I've got an inkling. I suspect it may be from a strange young man I've been seeing called Curtis—"

She turned to Barbara. "This meeting's confidential, right? Can I use his name?"

"Go ahead."

"He's called Curtis Pierson."

"Well," said Dharia slowly, "it *is* from Curtis Pierson."

Katrina frowned. "How do you know?"

"Because the first letter of each line spells out that name. Except for an F in the middle. Is that his middle initial?"

"Shit, Dharia, why didn't I see that? Damn! I think I was overreacting like Barbara said and didn't notice. He doesn't have a middle initial, at least not in his record or that he uses, but he did once tell me in confidence his middle name was...well, suffice to say it starts with an F. How could I have been so dumb? Shit! Of course, it only makes me feel slightly better. He likes to play games with me, and he likes word tricks. Look at his e-mail address. I read it at first as 'glockenspiel'—the musical instrument. But why the 'en' on the end, and the ampersand?"

Bill Denny, who was about to retire, fancied himself as a man of the world. "Maybe it is Glock, the pistol, and play— *spielen* in German. Disguised to make you think something benign rather than something sinister, like playing with a pistol. It's not real clever, but it might link up to the 'shoot to kill' line. Does he think he's a genius, by any chance?"

"Yeah, I'd say he does. But I think he *is* genuinely clever. He's a straight A student and he does no damn work at all. I wouldn't have expected him to make a common spelling mistake."

Having a strong idea who had written the e-mail, which was now seen as falsely anonymous and therefore less threatening, settled Katrina down. Her colleagues agreed she should wait until his next appointment and then ask Curtis to explain himself. As she drove home, she began to regret the agreement. It was all very well for them—Curtis wasn't their client sending them dark messages. It wasn't only her safety she was fearful for, what about the campus? Something that would cause an outrage from the public? And as a well-trained professional, she couldn't help thinking also that if Curtis was telling her that therapy was useless, could it indicate he was suicidal?

Katrina was on edge. It was going to spoil her entire week. She had a responsibility if he was having suicidal ideation and might shoot himself. She had no appetite, so she didn't make dinner. In any case, she was going to make a big dinner for Wednesday when Jeremy was coming over—she had promised him her famous chicken paprikash. She opened a bag of comforting caramel popcorn and a bottle of zinfandel. After her second glass, she knew she had to call Curtis, much as she hated doing so. You just never knew how he was going to react: sarcasm, silly game, hostility, or obsequiousness. But much as he bothered her, she knew he intrigued her—he was a whole lot more interesting than any of her other clients. And beneath his constant bullshit, there were flashes of perceptiveness.

She went to her purse and took out the cell phone the counseling center had allocated to her. It allowed her to make calls to clients without revealing her own private personal cell phone number. If anyone called this cell phone and it wasn't answered, the recorded message was from the center receptionist, asking the caller to leave a voice mail, but giving some information about the crisis hotline, the county emergency mental health team, and the hospital ER number to use if it was an emergency. Katrina let it ring for a while. There was no answer. She was about to hang up when an answer machine or service or something came on saying "You have reached a private number. At the tone, please leave a message."

"Hi Curtis, this is Katrina. I'm just calling to make sure you are okay. I had a few concerns about you, and as you know, I am always trying to support you. If you like, you can call me back at this number for another hour—oh, it's 9:30 pm on Monday right now in case your answering machine doesn't record time—but after about 10:30 you will not be able to reach me. I do hope everything is well. I'll see you later in the week at our usual time. But come in sooner if you need to. Bye, Curtis, have a good evening."

She thought maybe she'd been just a little too sugary. Asking him to have a good evening if he was suicidal wasn't sensible. The trouble was she was on her third glass of wine. She hoped her speech didn't sound slurry. Ugh, screw it. I'll watch some TV and forget about young Curtis. Fat chance. She knew she was in for a sleepless night, despite the zinfandel.

Curtis meantime, who was at home, played the recorded message over a few times, listening to her voice. 'Concerned. Support.' Nice words. He put his hand down his pants and pictured her, naked in front of her window. It was as clear in his mind's eye as though she was standing in front of him now. Clear too, her climbing the ladder to her loft bedroom. He rubbed himself. 'Concerned. Support.' The recording was repeating again. 'I hope everything is well.' *Put it in me Curtis. I want you. Yes, that's good. Ride me hard.* What a lovely voice she had on the tape, softer than usual, less prim. *Oh my god, Curtis, you're amazing.* It didn't take long. Curtis got up to get a few tissues.

Chapter 20: The Green-Eyed Monster

Curtis by now had his routine behind Katrina's barn apartment well established. He hated having to park so far away and walk to her place, especially with his fucked-up ankle. But the weather was improving, and there'd been no rain for a while. He was more careful not to leave footprints and kept well out of sight until reaching his favorite tree. The days were getting longer and it was lighter outside now.

Unfortunately, Katrina was not particularly reliable in her habits. One Friday evening she had been out and came home late. She didn't eat anything. She must have been out for dinner. Better not be with some guy. She had other things to do obviously and sometimes—days he felt most angry—she dressed in her night clothes in the bathroom with the door closed. But there were some spectacular successes as well, and Curtis now had clear images ingrained in his mind of her gorgeous breasts. Sometimes he was just happy watching her potter around doing odd jobs, and sometimes he just fantasized him there with her doing them together.

This evening she was obviously cooking up a storm. She'd spent a lot of time chopping something on a cutting board, fortunately in a bra and panties, which was some compensation. But when she set her little dining table with plates and napkins and candles, he realized something was up. Christ, she was having a visitor. Maybe it was another chick; maybe she was a lesbian and he'd have a seat in the front row of the royal circle to watch. But he sort of knew that she wasn't—he was confident he could always tell which women were gay.

Katrina hastily pulled on a dress, checked her hair in the mirror and a few moments later ushered in a man Curtis had never seen before. At the top of the stairs up to the studio, Katrina gave him a hug. Fuckin' hell. It had never occurred to Curtis she might have a boyfriend or a lover. For a moment he thought what it might be like to see them doing it up in her loft, or maybe in the candlelight on her large sofa. But as soon as that thought crossed his mind, he felt the most intense feeling of outrage he had had for a long time. What right had this prick to be there, in her apartment, obviously there for one purpose? Katrina had opened a bottle of wine, and they were both standing, looking out, drinking from large wine glasses.

Curtis couldn't stand it for another minute. The moment their backs were turned, he clambered down out of the tree and sneaked away down the side of the barn. He knew he just couldn't bear the thought, far less the sight, of Katrina with another man. He saw a new car parked outside. He walked, still hobbling, all the way to his own car. He returned with a hunting knife. He reached around and stuck it hard into the side of the rear tire, and then did the same to the inside wall of the opposite front tire. They did not deflate noticeably. Great. Maybe if they blow out at about the same time it will cause a major crash. The car was a front-wheel drive. Good. If the idiot guy panicked and braked he could have a serious spin, especially if he was on the highway. It would be up to the guy if he had enough skill to handle the emergency, and if he didn't, he deserved the consequences. Serve him right for trying to romance the beautiful Katrina Moss.

Back at home, it was hard for him to shake off his rage. He couldn't even explain why it bothered him so much. He smoked a joint. It didn't help, so he took two of the minor tranquilizers Dr. Abidi had prescribed. Curtis preferred the Tegretol, but Abidi was adamant that was the wrong medicine for him. "Let's just try the Xanax for a couple of weeks and see how you feel about it. Just .25 mg at first, three times a day. We'll monitor it. It will help with agitation." Right now, it was not. Curtis drank some vodka to give the Xanax a kick-start. For someone who knew just about everything, his pharmacology understanding was suspect.

Katrina had suggested he try writing his thoughts and feelings down. She called it something like 'narrative therapy'. Now was a good time to vent his hostility. Maybe make a plan to do something spectacular. Perhaps something that would make the whole university sit up and take notice of him. Something that would link him forever with Katrina Moss, Psychology Intern. Curtis went to his computer and started typing. His first sentence was 'The story of Curtis Pierson, Archangel of Vengeance.' He deleted that and wrote instead 'Raguel Battles Psychiatry for Man's Soul.'

He didn't get far. The vodka was making him fuzzy. He started thinking more about his own psychiatrist filling his blood stream with chemicals. What was Ali Baba up to? Was he ISIS? Probably. Was 'KFC' a code word for terrorist activity? Why was it crossed out? Curtis wrote some more rambling pages. A plan. Ideas were beginning to form. He didn't have it all figured out, but he had something definitive to work from. On the weekend he would oil his Glock.

Chapter 21: Crisis

It was now Tuesday morning. Katrina had gotten her coffee at Starbucks as usual and treated herself to a blueberry muffin, but she was not in a good space. Curtis hadn't shown up for his appointment on Friday and was not returning her calls. Jeremy's visit the previous week had been a nice distraction, and although he stayed the night, the evening had not gone all that well. It was her own fault, she realized, because she had been obsessing over one of her current patients, whom she had called 'PC', reversing his initials and smirking that he was about the least PC person she had ever encountered. She talked about her concerns far too much. Jeremy was patient and attentive. He had been sympathetic, but he knew little about the field of psychology. He was a lawyer. She had met him as a grad student at a party in Fenton, and they had been close for a year or more, but then he had to move to Albany, and he wasn't able to see much of her. They had drifted a little apart. He wasn't a criminal lawyer; he was writing bills for the New York State Assembly on regulating the use of plastic bags in supermarkets, and other green projects.

Yet he knew enough to express concern when Katrina mentioned her former professor thought PC could be dangerous. Maybe she should be more willing to consider reporting these concerns to the police? Jeremy had encountered the Tarasoff case in law school, and he was clear the Supreme

Court had upheld the safety of the community over the individual's right to confidentiality. Katrina hadn't wanted to be reminded of this, and she'd looked up a few other ethical cases over the weekend. She was back to worrying.

That was not a good emotional context for receiving a major shock. Ali Abidi burst into her office without knocking. He was wide-eyed and shaking, holding a crumpled sheet of paper in his hand.

"It's happening Katrina, you must contact your Security Committee right away. Curtis has snapped."

"Oh my God, what's happened? What's going on?"

He handed her the piece of paper, and sat down hard on one of her chairs. He was breathing heavily.

"Look at this. It's like a confession or something. I can't understand it all. Some of it seems psychotic, word salad. I've just found it. He must have dropped it. He was seeing me last week, and as he stood up to go, he dropped his backpack. It was open at the top and a whole lot of papers came out. He cursed— you know how foulmouthed he can be—and started to gather them up, and I bent down to help him and he literally pushed me away, snapping something like 'Leave it.' I backed off, and he stuffed everything into his backpack again and literally ran out. But this morning, half under my desk, I came across this sheet. He must have missed it. Here, have a read."

The paper looked like it had come from a printer, without much effort to correct spelling mistakes or typos, adding punctuation or capitals:

Manifesto. I Curtis Pierson am ready to wield the instruments of justice. By the time you read this you will know that the students on this campus have disrespected me for the last time. Not all deserve to die but none are innocent. I burn with desire to avenge my mother's incarceration and torture in the hands of evil people. Never disrespect the power of the bullet to make amends to enforce the unenforceable. The headlines will read doomsday at the university library. Carnage at five. Shooter escapes. Helter Skelter lives. Just no one thing. Analysis is futile Autopsy impotent. Understnading evades mini minds and small pathetic people, especially the police. This was not ISIS. This was pure American justice, the successor of the lynch mob, the extension of the electric chair, heir to the torturers at Gitmo. Americ's pride in justice is mired in sensless killing. How different am I? You will never know. 9/11 and 5/4—days to remember. Days to mourn. Days to recognize the mysteries of the minds of determined men...

It looked like the last sentence was not the end, but the corner and last little bit of the page appeared to have been torn off.

"I'm reading it a second time, Ali, but I'm puzzled. It doesn't sound anything like Curtis or anything he's said to me recently. He doesn't hate the students here—he despises the stupid ones, but many of them admire his talking out in classes. I do know the incarceration and suicide of his birth mother hangs over him like a terrible burden, but why he carries any guilt for that I don't know."

"I can explain. He hinted to me that he shot his father as a child and his mother was convicted of murder to protect him. He has a violent past and a terribly abusive childhood. We've been thinking of him as a personality disorder; but if he's

162

borderline, it would not be unusual for him to have a psychotic break. He's exactly the age for a first episode of schizophrenia."

It didn't make any sense to Katrina; why hadn't Curtis told her these things? But Ali's passion and confidence were convincing. He was the doctor, after all, and the psychiatrist. He must have dealt with dangerous people before. Maybe this item did look a bit like a practice at a confession of sorts. Cho at Virginia Tech had left rambling confessions, too, mainly on his computer. Katrina remembered the details. But if mass shooters were suicidal, it made sense they would attempt to leave a message. What about the new revelation from Ali? Hadn't Dave Gordon reminded her that past behavior was one of the surest ways to predict future behavior? Every psychologist knew that mantra. And now here was Dr. Abidi telling her that Curtis had killed his own father and was dangerous.

She knew now she had to alert the security team and the campus police as per their new procedures. Ali agreed. Using the special group number of #009, she sent a quick text. It was imperative the team should meet as soon as possible this morning. She had an alert. A dangerous situation was developing on campus. They needed to respond to it urgently.

"Ali, I should get Barbara to come along with me—she's my supervisor."

"But she's on record as not considering Curtis a threat. I'll go with you to emphasize this breach of confidentiality is a joint decision."

Half an hour later the entire security committee was finally assembled in the meeting room of the campus police office.

"This took far too long to get the Unified Incident Command Team together," Roger MacDonald, chairperson, grumbled.

"Jesus, DB, we have day jobs you know. I had to find some poor TA to take over my morning lecture class," Marcia Kastanowicz explained with feeling. "Next crisis had better not be on a Tuesday morning."

"It's no joking matter, Marcia. Katrina has come along with Dr. Abidi—I think you all know him—to report on a dangerous client. He has made one veiled threat and now one explicit one. And Ali and Katrina have figured out that whatever it is he intends to do, and it sure looks like a shooting incident because we know he owns a gun, will take place in the library at five o'clock this afternoon when it is packed with students who are enticed to actually read or at least check out a book by the promise of free doughnuts."

"Anyway," Roger continued after a pregnant pause, "I think the first thing we need to do is alert the Fenton police and have them come and take care of it, as they are better equipped, since Gary's team don't yet have semi-automatics—"

Gary Finch bristled. "Not a good idea, professor. This is our campus and our security problem. We're gonna handle it ourselves, believe me. And as to equipment, we certainly do all have semi-automatic assault rifles. President Michaels authorized their purchase for us two weeks ago, and we have had some rigorous training at a rifle range over by the airport."

"Damn it to hell, Gary, that's what I hate about autocrats and dictators who ask us to make a reasoned recommendation and then don't bother to wait for it and just go ahead and do it behind our backs. Son of a bitch. I'm willing to bet it was you, Gary, who initiated the end run."

"I did. And I'd do it again. I ain't apologizing. This committee wasn't about to make a recommendation any time soon. We were deadlocked and doing what a lot of professors do, which is talking hot air and not getting anything done. And thank God, too, because now we are ready for this crazy person. What's his name?"

"Curtis. Curtis Pierson."

Katrina felt she had to be the one to do it. There is a critical moment when you reveal something deeply private about a client who has been promised confidentiality, albeit with the usual provisos and assurances. This was that moment. No going back.

"He's..." she hesitated for a moment, "a psychopath who loves guns apparently and owns a handgun. He *is* potentially dangerous. I've got his phone number and his address. I've not yet tried to contact him, but I thought I could do so now and put him on speaker."

She picked up her phone and called Curtis's number. No answer. When his answering service kicked in, Katrina said as calmly as she could muster, "Hi Curtis, this is Katrina. Hope you get this message soon. It's very important I speak with you. You can call back on this number or call the clinic, but you must respond and we must see you. Thanks. Bye."

"I've also got his car license plate number, and his car is a black SUV with tinted windows—it's a Range Rover, probably about eight years old. He was proud of the fact it was an adventurer's car, not a Toyota or a Honda, which are strictly for suburban housewives. He likes to think of himself as a tough guy, but an intellectual one, more of an Indiana Jones than a Rambo—"

She was interrupted by Gary calling his police officers and giving them the information: "Do not radio out the car rego. If we broadcast it, the Fenton police might pick him up, not us, and not know how dangerous he is."

At this point in the discussion, Roger felt he had to take back some control as chair of the team. He didn't want to flatly contradict the doctor and Katrina, but he was getting worried at how their certainty was now defining the situation—creating the narrative. He had always thought Katrina was careful and cautious, but now she appeared to be reckless and panicking. They were still operating on little direct evidence. Comparison with fictitious movie characters was irrelevant as well as unscientific.

"Now hold on everyone," Roger blurted out, "we still do not know exactly how dangerous he is. We have bits and pieces of sort of second-hand information about threatening things he's written, and we have the clinical judgment of two people I respect without question, but we shouldn't get carried away. Aren't people in this country innocent until proved guilty, and are we not wary about insinuating that we know someone is likely to commit a crime, even though they have not yet done so? Are we lurching toward some sort of first strike idea here?"

"I agree with Roger," Marcia started, but Gary again interrupted.

"I don't care who agrees with who. Now this is a police matter, the decisions are mine. I've got the authority as a sworn law enforcement officer of the State of New York, and from now on things will be done my way. Give me his address again

166

Miss Moss, and we'll see if we can pick him up. If we don't know where he is, the attention must shift to preparing the campus for an attack at five p.m. in or near the library."

"That seems extremely sensible to me," Ali Abidi responded, "but now I have to go back to the health center. With Katrina over here, there needs to be someone in the clinic who knows what is going on in case he does show up there. It's somewhere familiar, where he's felt safe in the past. And he might well have second thoughts and come in for help. Anyway, I'm not a member of this group so I am going to take my leave, but you can reach me any time if I'm needed. I just must emphasize again he's unpredictable, probably armed, and extremely paranoid. He recently came up with some bizarre fantasy that Chief Finch here is an active member of a lunatic fringe white supremacy group here in town. Please be careful."

As Dr. Abidi left, Finch suddenly got to his feet, muttering something about briefing his officers who were going to Curtis's address. Outside the room, he pulled two of his men aside and hissed at them with urgency.

"Listen up, now we know for sure this psycho kid is the one who came to our meeting, the STAND meeting. He fuckin' recognized me. He probably recognized the two of you as well. That's bad, real bad. If he's home when you go to his house, you'll know what to do. He's violent and dangerous. The shrink made it clear to us. Don't take any chances, understand? One more thing, if you don't find him we have another chance to take him down—however we plan it, the two of you will be in a good position. I guarantee it. Now get out there and find the little fucker."

Fenton is a small town. It was only a matter of minutes before Finch received the call from his officers. "He's not home," Gary Finch reported to the worried group. "They broke in, but found nothing. We'd better get back to a focus on the library."

With attention shifting to prevention of an attack on the library, they had a little more time to plan. President Michaels was informed of the situation by Tonya and advised to cancel his Council meeting that afternoon. He said he'd think about it, but to keep him informed as to any additional developments. Roger and Gary gave him a further update a little later. Roger called Susan and alerted her as well; he decided not to inflame political strife by mentioning the campus police were now heavily armed, thanks to Michaels. Maybe she knew already, but he doubted it. Susan was one of the most honest and transparent university administrators he had ever encountered. Katrina was being quiet, no doubt all her insecurities and professional inexperience were fighting her rational self. Dave Gordon had encouraged her to think actuarially—to assess the probabilities coldly and in terms of specific behavior patterns. That was what she was trying to do. She now had evidence of a threat, and, even more importantly, evidence of Curtis having a violent past.

Finch produced a detailed campus map, and they all studied their options. There were basically only two ways into the library for anyone not a librarian coming in from outside. Roger wanted to clear the library and warn the students and faculty, but Gary Finch, Phil Cohen, and Karl Goga were dead set against that. It would cause panic, they said. If Pierson was around he could take advantage of it. If not, he'd simply postpone his plan to later, and they would have to deal with the same crazy situation all over again.

"Fuck," said Roger, who was getting increasingly agitated, "I thought our goal was prevention of an incident, and here you lot are planning the friggin' gunfight at O.K. Corral. How do you think you will be able to keep students safe if you have some kind of Hollywood shoot out?"

There was further discussion, and Finch outlined his proposal, which was a sort of trap. His officers would arrive some time before five with their assault rifles hidden as much as possible, get all students and library staff out of the front foyer of the library, and have a lockdown of everyone in the library. They would then place themselves strategically for when Curtis came into the foyer and challenge him to drop flat to the ground, spread-eagled with his arms stretched out.

"What if he's already in the library? Worse still, what if he comes to the library around five with all the other people arriving at that time?" Roger asked. "Apparently lots come for the free food."

"We can cordon off the entrance and quietly turn away other students. I'll have one of my officers in plain clothes there to do that. We've got his mug shot from campus records. My guy won't challenge Curtis if he sees him, but he'll alert us on our intercom earphones. It's not foolproof, let's face it, but it is our best chance to isolate him and take him out."

"Good God, Finch, there you go again. I hope that was a slip of the tongue, and you meant arrest him and search him and read him his Miranda rights..."

Finch laughed out loud. "Of course—we'll treat him so gently you'd be amazed."

The heavy sarcasm finally provoked Katrina, who erupted angrily: "I agree with Roger. There must be some additional warning. Can't we send out Curtis's picture to all student cellphones with a simple message that the police are looking for him; do not approach but text the following number yada yada yada? It might alert him, but that is largely what we want."

Finch just sneered at her.

Roger tried another direction. "With at least two possible ways into the library we know about, you guys are going to get no warning of when he's coming in and where. If we could place other officers in plain clothes at the entrances, you'd have better information."

"How many officers do you think we have, *professor*? Two of my men are on leave, and one is in the hospital with suspected appendicitis. I've got five guys, including myself. No, we'll be in place ahead of time, and we'll neutralize anyone who comes in whatever goddamned door they—he, Curtis—chooses."

Roger was getting increasingly desperate. He could sense where this was leading, and they were running out of time. Katrina was looking at him pleadingly as she, too, recognized where all this was going, and the look made him particularly determined. He wanted to protect her from being the direct cause of the assassination or maybe suicide by police of one of her clients who had put his trust in her professional skills. Sort of. Curtis didn't sound like someone who trusted anybody. Roger had now been given a mental picture of a dangerous killer with a mental disorder, and he thought of all the recent cases—Aurora, Charleston, Sandy Hook. He was extremely agitated and quite out of his depth. Then he thought of the one thing he knew best. He suddenly logged onto the police office computer, went to his own Cloud account and pulled up a detailed schematic of the drains and tunnels under the campus.

"Look here everyone. There is an easy access to the library complex from one of the main underground tunnels. There's a waterproof hatch to prevent flooding into the library basement that can be opened from inside the drain; I've got the key. It comes up here, see, on the library map. That means someone, probably me since I'm the only one who knows the way, could place themselves unseen in this storage room well before five and be able to observe exactly where anyone is entering—that closet door has a reinforced glass panel. It's a while since I've used that access to the drains, but I've been in and out of there a few times in the past. I'd send a text to all of you on our new secure emergency system. Since Curtis will not be expecting anyone to know where he's coming in, even if he picked up the proposed campus-wide alert, the element of surprise will enable you to confront him and arrest him without excessive force."

They all stared at the complex map of drains and dark tunnels like a massive infestation of deranged moles beneath the thriving open activity of a busy campus.

Finally Finch spoke, "Well, it's not for nothing they call you Drain Brain, Professor. It's a wild idea, but it might just work. It really might. In any case, it would be helpful if we could focus our limited manpower on the specific access route this creep will be taking. Yeah, very helpful indeed. You would be our eyes and give us time to respond appropriately."

Roger relaxed a smidgen, not recognizing that 'appropriately' could be taken a few different ways. Katrina smiled at him and leant across and gave his arm a squeeze.

"Thank God for some sanity around here," she whispered in his ear. He was encouraged.

Chapter 22: Keep Calm and Carry On

Jack Michaels, fifth president of the Chenango Valley State University—second in size only to the Stony Brook campus in the state system—received the terrifying news of a dangerous shooter on campus with remarkable composure and a strong sense of purpose. This vindicated his decision to authorize greater firepower for the campus police as well as his decision to form a campus security committee that could shoulder some responsibility for the situation and share the blame if things went belly up. No one would later be able to say he was caught with his pants down. Yes, the faculty, and indeed most students, had resisted his appointment, scorned his military accomplishments, and derided his years of successful leadership. Pretentious academic snobbery. But he'd had the foresight to create a faculty and staff committee and had given them some authority over possible crises, and now they could face the same test of their guts as he had faced over and over in Iraq.

Forewarned is forearmed. He would not take full command until more was known. That was why he had collaborated with Finch, whom he instinctively didn't like but knew he needed, and had won his total support and loyalty with the assault rifle deal. It was up to Finch now to handle things. And he wasn't

173

going to cancel his own important meetings. They were confident the threat was to the library; his office was on the other side of campus. If you run around hysterically and cancel everything, then terrorists win. They want to create fear and disruption. Stand your ground, he thought to himself, show no fear, and don't cower from threats. Most terrorists, especially domestic terrorists, crave recognition—this was why it was always stupid of the TV news and the papers to constantly publicize the faces of staring-eyed lunatics, tattooed criminals, and flag-toting, Toyota-driving jihadists who had decided mass shootings were the way to achieve fame.

Finch and MacDonald had given him an additional quick briefing him on what little they knew about Curtis Pierson. A psychopath. The psychologists and the psychiatrists had drawn up a profile on him. Classic background, abusive, alcoholic father abandoned by a mother who might now be dead, raised by foster parents, working class. Adoptive father had died of a heart attack; his adoptive mother blamed stress caused by the great recession of 2008. She was bitter and depressed. She managed a bowling alley in the strip mall on the rough side of the river. It was a job, but paid half of what she'd been earning as a cashier at Sears, which had closed after posting two years of losing revenue. Money was tight and she was angry—blamed Obama. Curtis had told her that was ridiculous—he was a smart boy, too smart for his own good. He'd done well at school, but was moody. Didn't have any girlfriends as far as anyone knew, although girls found him attractive. Frustrated sexuality was a potent force—didn't one of those previous campus shooters complain he couldn't get a girl to go to bed with him?

Michaels was told how this Curtis fellow had worked hard at two different part-time jobs, bought himself a used Range Rover, and moved to his own cheap apartment when he started college. His mom admired him, and that boosted his self-esteem. But they had a distant relationship, lacking warmth. Little attachment. To Jack Michaels, it seemed like a textbook problematic background from what he remembered of his undergraduate days in a fourth-year class on abnormal psychology. On the other hand, it wasn't that different a background from hundreds of other young men he'd encountered in the army—daredevils who made recklessly efficient soldiers but were quick to beat up harmless villagers who wouldn't toe the line. It didn't make them domestic terrorists. The whole thing could be a false alarm, but a good test of the new emergency procedures.

No need to cancel his monthly meeting. At three-thirty, his Council meeting would begin, and some of his top administrators would be there, certainly the provost, whom he wasn't certain could be trusted, along with one or two of the vice-presidents and members of the University Council. Sometimes some of those lazy bums didn't show up to meetings, but Michaels didn't care. He always had his PA call a few and remind them about the meeting and send them their parking passes. But she reminded only those members of the Council whom he could tell liked him, and he was sure were the ones who'd supported his candidacy late last year. It was always a lot easier to get things done if you had friends on any committee. Of course, he would tell them about the crisis about to unfold on the other side of campus, but he would demonstrate his faith in his own security measures by not locking down the entire admin building.

The Council meeting was due to end at five anyway, and if there were still any threats out there, he could simply ask them all to stay. The big official conference room had solid doors that could be locked from the inside. They would be quite safe. It was obvious that the security team knew a lot about this Curtis fellow: where he lived, what some of his movements were. It should be easy to respond to the man's threats. Evidently every one of Jack's subordinates were pulling together and he needn't worry.

Some of his confidence was self-deceptive, however. Ever since coming to Fenton and the new job, and facing such strong opposition, the one thing Jack Michaels worried about was how much his autocratic style was nothing but a front. He didn't enjoy violence, and a part of his war experience in the Middle East had effectively shattered his life and damaged his military reputation back in Baghdad. Sometimes the indiscriminate bombing—Christ, the Air Force had even flattened a hospital run by Doctors Without Borders and refused to take responsibility—saddened him beyond bearing. The details were like pictures in his mind, photographic 'flashbulb' images, flashbacks, memories so vivid he still couldn't think of them without intense sadness.

Projecting toughness was the only possible antidote to this pain that he knew.

Chapter 23: Down the Rabbit Hole and into the Drains

The moment Roger lowered himself into the main manhole and down the upright iron steps built into the cylindrical slimy green wall, he realized that this was an extremely bad idea. He had plenty of time, about ninety minutes, to make his way towards the extra-large drain that had been built to protect the library stacks from any further flooding. It contained a waterproof hatch, like in a submarine, which then led directly into one of the archive rooms. From there, a seldom-used staircase led up to a first-floor storage area. This allowed a silent and undetectable vantage point, regardless of what sneaky direction Curtis might approach the foyer from to access the main reference reading room with its banks of computers and a couple of hundred students finishing assignments, reading, whispering loudly to each other, sleeping, staring at their cellphones. The storage room door, he knew, had a reinforced glass panel so one could see if anyone was behind it before swinging it wide open. From there, Roger could survey the entire scene and detect Curtis's movements, which he'd then relay to the eager team under the command of Chief Finch. Even if Curtis was already somewhere in the library watching the front area, he would never know he'd be under surveillance from the little storage room.

It had sounded good in the campus security command post, but there were obvious things that could go horribly wrong. The watertight hatch might not be so easy to open. There could be a flash flood—the very thing the drains were designed to accommodate. Naturally they had checked the weather and it was unlikely, but not impossible. Or he might trip and fall and break a leg—Roger was not as fit or as supple as he should be. One of the campus security officers had volunteered for the mission, but he'd have gotten lost for sure, even if he had a blueprint. Roger was the only one who knew the way. And as to the campus police themselves—the 'swat team' Finch was now calling them—they were more like Keystone Cops, as Fenton police officer Joe Stiglioni had warned during the first meeting. God knows whom they might shoot with their shiny new toys.

But then the worst situation of all, one they stupidly hadn't thought of, happened. As he moved cautiously down the tunnels in dank wonderland, he checked his cell phone. Fuck fuck fuck. His smart phone indicated 'No signal'. How could that be? He tried sending a text and then he tried 911— emergency calls are given priorities in most systems. Nothing. Stupid idiot. It was obvious. During the design of the new drain system for the campus, extra reinforcing had been installed. And above him were various labs which were shielded to protect experiments from unwanted radio signals. That might be it. All he had to do was keep going, and soon he'd find a spot where there was normal reception.

Why had he done this alone? He could easily have shown one or more campus police officers the way. But there was the risk of greater noise, someone sneezing or coughing. Surprise

178

and being undetectable was the key to this part of the whole plan. And Finch had insisted he needed all his men posted inside the library, with maybe one out of uniform just by the main entrance. But if Roger had had just one companion, that person could have run back and told someone about the lack of cell phone coverage. Hmm, no one would be back there anyway at the campus police office in the admin building, the George Pataki Building. Everyone was now staking out the library, needing to be in position on that side of the campus before five. So there it was. He needed to be brave and press on.

Roger put his cell phone carefully back in the front pocket of his cargo pants. His pants now had wet patches from the dampness of the drain, and his shirt was wet with sweat, even though it was cold down there in the dark. The tunnel he was now in was a low and narrow one, and he had to crawl along it—slowly, because he still had plenty of time, and slipping and breaking something was the last thing he needed, especially now he knew there was no cellphone coverage at this particular location, maybe nowhere down in this smelly, uninviting maze of damp and fetid concrete.

He inched past a smaller side tunnel and pointed his flashlight down it. Six, maybe ten, feet away, in the surprisingly weak beam of the LED, he saw the bars of a sturdy iron gate. It was one of about five gates that had been built into the system, basically to stop just exactly what he was doing: someone crawling around below the university and up to no good. They also served as useful traps for any larger item of debris that might get swept down in a serious flood. Excellent. It was exactly where it should be. He had not gotten disoriented or confused. The side tunnel was perfectly dry. Good place to sit and rest a bit and try again to see if he could send an emergency text on the smartphone, even though he couldn't make a call. He plonked himself down next to the gate, his right arm lightly touching the cold metal and his left hand fishing in his trouser pocket for his phone. Suddenly, out of the darkness, something gripped his wrist and held it like an alien force.

Chapter 24: The Psychopath

It was a moment of pure terror. "What the fuck!" Roger yelled in a high-pitched voice, and reflexively tried to pull his arm away from next to the gate. But the grip held. He had the sensation his bowels were turning to water, and he felt the hair on the back of his neck stand up, the first time in his life he had experienced it. Not thinking rationally, he simply wanted to get away from this inhuman, vice-like grip, and he knew nothing or no-one could hold onto his wrist if he simply wrenched his whole body as far from the gate as he could. But as he raised his knees to plant his feet on the ground and make his dash, a chilling voice echoed off the dark, dank walls of the tunnel.

"Move a muscle, old man, and I'll blow your fucking head off."

Roger peered at the gate. He'd dropped his flashlight in his moment of surprise, but in the dim light it still offered lying on the floor of the drain he could see the silvery-black glint of steel from what was unmistakably the muzzle of a handgun, pointed through the bars right at him. Roger froze. It was easy enough to do—millions of years of evolution have shaped our most primitive neural responses when in dire threat to flee, fight, or freeze. And in this situation only one of these was an option.

"Very slowly, pick up your flashlight and shine it in your face."

Thinking that having the flashlight back in his hand might give him just the tiniest edge, Roger complied.

"Jesus Christ, you're Drain Brain!" came the response. "How superbly ironic, especially as I nearly spilled what brains you have in this lovely drain. Which I might still do, since the poetry of it appeals to me."

What was still left of Roger's cortical functioning, not overwhelmed by his limbic system, was working, but barely. His mouth was so dry he wasn't sure any words would come out, but surely talking was a good thing—if this maniac was going to shoot him, he could easily have done so by now. Time to take a small risk.

"I hope you won't do that Curtis. I don't know what you are doing behind that gate, but I know for a fact it's locked, and just maybe I have the key."

Roger sensed he had hit a nerve—the pressure on his wrist became still tighter. If it was Curtis, he had an amazingly strong grip. There was a moment of profound silence, before the voice hissed:

"How the fuck do you know my name?"

"How the fuck did you know mine?"

"Because I took a god-awful boring class from you last year, and during the brief time when I wasn't sleeping, I had to stare at your ugly old-man face. And since you never made eye-contact with me the entire semester, and since you haven't done so down here, let me repeat: how the fuck do you know my name?"

Roger was still desperately trying to think what to do. All he knew about Curtis was that he was a raging psychopath. He didn't want to annoy him and he didn't want to risk bullshitting

182

him, so without drama and with a faint sigh of the inevitable, he replied:

"Because everyone across this whole goddamned campus is looking for you now they know you're a dangerous extremist. Your mug shot is about to be plastered across every university computer, and in slightly less than an hour, your photo will be in everyone's e-mail, faculty and students—"

"Fuckin' idiots!" Curtis responded and then fell silent, obviously thinking, but what?

Roger waited and then tried again. "Then what exactly are you doing down here Curtis? You are rather trapped I'd say. This gate is locked, and you'll have to go back the way you came. All I need to do is jerk my wrist out of your slowly fading grip and crawl down this tributary to the main tunnel, and I'm out of here."

"Don't get any ideas, professor. Move an inch and I'll shoot you dead. I'm serious."

"Maybe, but you might miss, and in any case, you wouldn't be able to get to my key which I obviously have."

"Don't be so sure, and don't try to be clever. Your dead body would still be within my reach, and I'd drag you back and get the key, which I'd guess is hanging on a lanyard, the one I saw around your neck when you lit up your terrified face for me."

"Ah, my key is important to you Curtis, and now I'm thinking again. I think I know why. The tunnel you are in, at least that side of the gate, drops down suddenly from another level. I'm guessing of course, but it seems entirely possible you lost your way, fell down that drop, and can't climb back up the smooth cement."

"Don't try to play games with me. I might just fucking shoot you right now, you smug shit."

Roger knew instantly from the tone of his voice that what he had described to Curtis was one hundred percent correct. He was trapped and wasn't denying it. But Roger was trapped too. He might get far enough away from the gate to stop Curtis getting his hands on the key, but he'd be dead for sure. Without the cell phone coverage, and off the main tunnels, it might be days before he was found, and Curtis might be dead too—maybe a fall had injured him in some way or maybe he'd just shoot himself after taking care of Roger. They were at an impasse. Of course, the attack on the library would not occur, Curtis's plan would have been foiled, and Roger, dead or alive, would be something of a hero. He knew at that instant he should make a run for it—throw himself as hard and as fast as he could down the tunnel. Maybe Curtis would miss or not hit a vital part. Curtis was well and truly trapped. The game was over. Roger allowed himself a moment of relaxation.

Curtis felt it and guessed what Roger was cooking up in his little drain brain. He adjusted his gun, pulling it back from the iron bars so it could not be wrenched from his hand, and let go Roger's wrist.

"I know what you're thinking, Professor. Go ahead and make your run, and I'll put six or more shiny bullets into your roly-poly body, what I'd call a soft target. Yo! When they come looking for you they'll let me out. I'll be the hero. I'll say I mistook you for a terrorist in the dark. I'll get a medal."

"Fat chance, Curtis. They know you are the campus shooter, you're the terrorist. That's why your face is plastered all over campus: 'Dangerous, do not approach, call campus security immediately.'"

There was a long silence. Although he couldn't see Curtis's face, Roger was sure now for the first time he'd be feeling vulnerable, a failure, plot foiled, a loser, an idiot who fell down a drain. How pathetic. How ignoble. The dangerous sociopath, terror of the campus, caught in a drain underground like the rat he was. What pathos.

But Curtis's reply, when it came, was unexpected. Weird, in fact.

"I don't know what shit you're talking about. I'm not the danger. I'm here to stop the danger. I'm here to stop the maniac who's going to kill the university's president."

"Okay," Roger replied without hesitation, "now I know you're a pathological liar as well as a sociopath. No one's going to kill the president—you were going to shoot people in the library. But we got a warning. Half the campus is on lock-down, or will be soon. You boasted it would be at five o clock. I was on my way through these tunnels to the underground entrance to the library building where I would be able to watch for you without being seen and text the information to the police sharp-shooters. You're finished, Curtis, no matter what happens next."

Roger could not suppress the little note of triumph in his voice, and it minimized the impact on him of what Curtis said next.

"Christ Jesus, you professors are even more stupid than you look and sound in class. Do you believe that shit? Obviously I've been framed. The plot is to kill the president and his senior management team. I was trying to find my way to the admin building to stop the crazy asshole. You'd better unlock this fucking gate right now, so I can stop him, especially as I'm sure your fucking cellphone isn't working any better than mine. Hurry up. There isn't much time; it must be getting close to five. You can show me the right tunnels, and then I won't fuckin' shoot you, maybe. At least not right away. Better open up, you dumb shit."

"Very funny Curtis; I know you think I'm stupid, but I'm not so stupid as to listen to a psychopath, a known pathological liar, spinning a fantastic story in a desperate attempt to get me to free him so he can shoot me and proceed on the library, for whatever crazy hate-filled reason and take out your rage on innocent students."

"You are way more stupid than I ever thought. I may be a psychopath, but I'm not a killer. Why would I be? Sure, I dislike some of the students, but I wouldn't waste bullets on them…"

"Then who's the real killer then, smarty pants, who wants to shoot President Michaels?"

There was another momentary pause and Roger wondered if Curtis was trying to conjure up a plausible villain—this cat and mouse game was getting increasingly bizarre.

"Doctor Abidi."

"Oh, that's rich—name the only poor Arab you can think of on campus, you racist bastard. Yeah, a distinguished doctor and campus psychiatrist—probably one you have had a lot of dealings with—is going to shoot the university president."

"I'm not sure if he's going to shoot him and the others. I think Abidi might be wearing a suicide vest. That's why I needed to approach the council board room undetected, so I could figure it all out and take him down before he could blow them all up, and me as well, quite likely."

"You've been watching way too many terrorist movies on TV. You're living in a sick fantasy world. Why would you be the savior of the situation, rather than simply pass such make-believe information on to campus security? And more importantly why did you think you could get to the admin building through these drains?"

"Because, you dimwit, no one would believe me for a minute. I do have a bad reputation. Abidi has a lot of power. He would have denied everything—he's clever—and move to have me committed as delusional, as paranoid. But if I stop him, I'm a hero. People will notice me—talk about me for years. Girls will want to date me. I'll be in the *New York Times*. On CNN. They'll probably give me a big financial reward. The president's fat wife will be so overcome with gratitude she'll beg to give me a blowjob.

"And as to knowing about drains, you were the pompous asshole that gave an entire lecture in class on drain design, using CVSU as an example. You showed us a schematic of the drains on your boring PowerPoints, and you showed us a video clip you had taken on the tunnels down here. For once I was paying attention as I was sure it would come in handy—and now it has.

"But none of this is going to happen if we sit here in the dark talking about it—I don't even have a six pack and a bag of Doritos to help pass the time during our little drain-side chat. Open this fucking gate right now and show me the underground way to the Pataki Building. I'll let you share in some of the glory if we don't both get blown to smithereens."

Roger could feel the nausea rising, dry mouth giving way to acidic bile. His head was aching. He was sweating profusely. He felt he was trapped in some sort of nightmare. How could he sit here, with a crazy killer, listening to him spin an inconceivable story about being framed by a well-known and reasonably distinguished member of the medical profession? It made no sense whatever. Yet Curtis, despite becoming more and more shrill and coarse, sounded more believable than Roger wanted to consider. Wasn't that a characteristic of psychopaths? They could lie with such facility—it was a symptom, wasn't it? Roger wished he'd paid a bit more attention to his friend, Dave Gordon, who would know about such things. He should have asked Katrina many more questions, but he was too besotted by her. What else might be important in judging plausibility? Motivation? Yes, of course. Curtis was caught like a weasel in a trap—he had all the motivation in the world to lie through his sharp evil teeth and to try to convince Roger to make the biggest mistake of his life.

Roger could have been thinking fast, like every super hero ever seen, a James Bond in a tight spot making brilliant snap decisions. Unfortunately, whether it was the stress or his innate cautiousness as an academic, always trying to present balance on issues to his students, Roger's brain was barely working at all. But through the fog, he suddenly realized that motivation could open another mental door.

"What possible motivation could Dr. Abidi have for wanting to kill President Michaels? Are you going to try to argue he's a member of ISIS or something?"

"I've no idea if he's a member of ISIS. He could be, but I suspect not. I only have a hint of an idea—maybe he didn't get promoted or get a raise. Isn't it always anger about being unfairly passed over that makes people go postal and kill their bosses? But let me put the question back to you: what possible motive would I have for killing students in the library? Christ, I barely know where the fuckin' library is—I get all my info online. I only go there for the doughnuts. Do you think I'd want to shoot up my doughnut supply?"

"You've just said you want the glory. You're a narcissist with a personality disorder who craves notoriety. You want to do something dramatic that will get attention, the same reason Hinckley tried to shoot Ronald Reagan, to impress a movie star he had a crush on."

"I've no idea what you are yakking on about old man. Reagan was long before my time. But I have no movie stars I want to impress."

"Maybe you have some sort of grudge against the students here, like the student at Virginia Tech who resented the student body for their wealth and their rejection of him."

"Fuck you, Drain Brain. The students here aren't wealthy, and far from rejecting me, they love me. The guys think I'm cool because I often challenge the faculty and their pseudo-liberal, phony PC views. If I had a grudge, it would be against people like you—so I'd go and shoot up a faculty meeting somewhere. But I don't. And in any case, crazy school and college shooters die in a hail of cops' bullets. I may be looking for fame but I'm not fucking suicidal. Why are we talking like this? You're wasting valuable time. Abidi's going to kill Michaels at exactly four fifty-five, unless you unlock this gate and guide me to the admin building."

"And how would a student like you know this? Did Dr. Abidi just happen to mention during one of your therapy sessions, 'Oh, by the way Curtis, I'm planning on blowing up the president of the university.' Eh?"

"Oh, stop being silly and sarcastic. I figured it out. I'm fuckin' smart. I found out some things about him, and I figured out what he was up to. I don't know why, but as I said, he must have some sort of grudge, maybe going back to his time in Iraq. He's got papers in his desk drawers that are official US army documents and a bunch of others in Arabic, all squiggly."

At that moment, Roger sensed he might well soil himself. His bowels felt like water. There was the oddest element to Curtis's practiced and strangely smooth diatribe—it had just the faintest ring of authenticity. It was far too fantastic to be made up on the spot. This was a defining moment. He tried hard to pull himself together. He closed his eyes and took a few breaths. How do you know when a practiced, pathological liar is telling the truth? He tried a tactic, one he'd often used in risky civil engineering situations: hypothesize the worst-case scenario and see where it led.

"If I believe you and I unlock the gate, what is stopping you from coming out here and shooting me anyway? It's lose-lose for me."

"Because, pea brain, not drain brain, don't you realize I'm fucking lost? I need you to show me the way through these horrid little tunnels to get to the admin building and there may be other barriers you'll know how to circumvent or unlock."

"Okay, what if you give *me* your gun. You stay locked up here so you can't massacre students in the library, and I'll make

190

my way to the Pataki Building and see if there is any sign of Dr. Abidi attacking a meeting…"

"And then what would you do? Shout 'hands up' and he replies 'Don't shoot'? You're shaking like a leaf as it is. Do you own a handgun?"

"No."

"Have you ever fired a gun?"

"No."

"Jesus, what a pussy. Even if Abidi doesn't show up, you'd probably shoot the fucking president yourself by mistake."

It was some combination of Curtis's humor and his open contempt for Roger and his rather unassailable logic that tipped the scales. What happened next tipped them just a little further.

"Okay, let me—" Roger began, but Curtis interrupted.

"Before we strike some sort of deal, there is one thing I want to know. You say the whole campus has been alerted I'm somehow going to attack the library. I realized the moment you said it that I'd been framed, but someone had to put that story out. Where did it come from? Was it from Dr. Abidi? It would be a devious way to ensure he could walk unquestioned into the boardroom with all of the security guys marshalled on the other side of campus. I've been a patient of Abidi's—it would be easy for him to stigmatize me with a psychiatric label."

"Well it wasn't him directly. It was another source, but she quoted Abidi who claimed to have seen something you had written gave details of the planned library shooting. I was part of an emergency briefing just a couple of hours ago, and she described you as a classic psychopath lacking empathy with callous disregard for others—"

"*She*? You said she? Who was it?"

"It was one of the counselors, Katrina Moss." As he said her name, Roger realized he'd made a terrible mistake.

Curtis erupted. "That fuckin' hateful immature bitch. She's my therapist. She's supposed to maintain confidentiality. She's supposed to be on my side, right or wrong, mad or sane. What a cunt. When this is over I'm going to bury her career. She'll never work as a psychologist ever again, believe me, I'll sue her 'til she's destitute."

Suddenly realizing this was his first genuine-sounding outburst, Curtis hastily added, "But I'd never hurt her. Destroying her career is fair, but not violence."

Oddly enough, he needn't have added any of that. The vehemence of Curtis's hurt feelings and sense of betrayal by someone he trusted was a sufficiently authentic moment of outrage to sound genuine to Roger. Maybe the first such moment. He only vaguely knew whether therapists and counselors and psychologists had some sort of duty to report threats of violence by their clients to try to prevent harm to others, but he had a sense they were supposed never to breach confidentiality, a bit like a lawyer, or a priest in the confessional.

Katrina had tried to be somewhat circumspect, but in the end she had spilled the beans on her client, blatantly calling him dangerous and unpredictable, with a fascination with guns, and a deep rage based on a troubled background. It had sounded convincing at the briefing, and as she answered questions she had warmed to her theme: Curtis Pierson was dangerous and was likely to cause great harm. He had written personal statements which had come into Dr. Abidi's hands—she didn't question how—and putting that together with all her own observations was the final confirmation of her judgment. Curtis would be the first mass shooter on the CVSU campus.

Roger thought his head would split open from the pressure and pain. He knew he could think nothing but desire for Katrina, who could do no wrong. In the meeting, he had not a shred of doubt regarding her wisdom and judgment, but now he could see the way evidence might get distorted with the tiniest manipulation by a respected doctor of medicine. Yes, the most damning documentation had come via Abidi. That was odd.

But he, Roger, was the one who had said we have to give the benefit of the doubt. *You must stand up for your own principles in life*, Roger thought. Curtis might be a raving lunatic and a devious liar, but fairness had to be considered, even if he was making a terrible mistake. There was only one way now to find out how terrible the mistake might be. Roger fumbled for the master key around his neck and, with his hands shaking, unlocked the iron gate. He moved out of the way as it swung towards him and Curtis Pierson, Glock in hand, clambered awkwardly out. Roger closed his eyes tight and braced himself for execution.

Chapter 25: Colonel Jacques

The US State Department official had been true to her word. It was not difficult for a well-placed aide to the Assistant Secretary in Washington to pull some strings. She didn't know for sure why the intelligence branch of the military was so keen to stop this doctor from constantly obsessing and pursuing the fate of his wife in Baghdad. Terrible things were happening in Iraq, and it wasn't clear why Dr. Abidi's personal horror was any worse than countless other terrible stories. For God's sake, the shock and awe campaign had left an estimated sixty thousand Iraqi civilians dead. Why was this man's wife more special than any of the other fifty-nine thousand, nine hundred and ninety-nine?

But she was efficient. Ali Abidi got his green card, and his medical qualifications were approved by the New York State Office of the Professions. Getting him Board Certified in Psychiatry without taking an exam and with a specialization certificate from Iraq was more complicated. But she did it. Finding a job for Ali was not hard at all. Psychiatrists were in short supply, especially in more rural areas, and his M.D. from a prestigious American university eliminated the usual concern that a foreign doctor wouldn't be able to understand the nuances of language and cognitive symptomatology essential for talking to adult mental patients. The final stage was a matter of luck. The Chenango Valley State University had just posted a job advert for a psychiatrist to work in the student health center. Ali got the job.

He liked the university and he got on reasonably with the other professionals. They trusted his knowledge of drugs and were willing to rely on his diagnostic conclusions, despite the ethos of the counseling program being more humanistic and against the disease model of mental disorders—after all some sort of diagnosis from the DSM had to be entered onto the insurance forms for those students who had their own health coverage. However, Ali's chronic dysphoria made it hard to include him in social events, and those who didn't know him well described him as standoffish. A couple of people tried to match him up with female friends and to see if they could encourage him to date. He was after all, good looking and kept himself trim and fit. But after some disastrous experiences, it became more widely known Dr. Abidi was still mourning the mysterious death of his wife in Iraq and was in no emotional shape to start any new romantic relationships. It was recognized by his professional colleagues in the health center that whatever healing he needed, he was preventing himself from experiencing the best possible way of overcoming grief such as his. What he needed was to find a sympathetic, caring, loving partner with whom he could share his feelings.

Ali didn't mind Fenton as a place to live. He could afford a pleasant house near the river, and this was an attractive part of upstate New York, although not as picturesque as some of the Finger Lakes towns, like Ithaca. The only thing that bothered him was that there were segments of the local population who were deeply suspicious of Arabs and Muslins generally. And with the crisis in Syria and the rise of ISIS worsening every day, the hostility was becoming more palpable. It didn't matter how often he told people he wasn't a Muslim and had no interest in religion. The associations were made wherever he went. This was one reason he'd taken such an instant dislike to Curtis Pierson. The only good thing about Curtis was that, miraculously, he had come along at the perfect moment.

Ali had spent many fruitless hours, in both formal correspondence and in informal Internet searches, trying to track down the mysterious Jacques Sanders or even the secret research center where Adilah had worked apparently happily for many months after they had returned to Iraq. It had become an obsession, but one that was fully contained by the complete lack of new information or leads. The most common image in his head was of a vicious army officer, called Sanders, perhaps with a cane, perhaps not, who could have been French, maybe from Syria.

Ali had not gone to any of the campus talks from the three contenders for the vacant president position. He wasn't keen on campus politics. He had an instinctive dislike for the candidate described as a general. When chatting to colleagues or anyone in the center kitchen area where they met for coffee or snatched a bite of lunch if they were busy with clients, he joined in the sense of outrage that the Council had appointed a military man, even if he had a Ph.D. But when Jack Michaels scheduled a sort of inaugural address to the faculty after a month in office, Ali thought he should go along and give the guy a fair chance.

When Jack Michaels was introduced by the chairperson of the Council as someone who had served with distinction as a colonel in the US Army intelligence services in Iraq, and this stocky figure walked slowly up to the podium leaning on a cane, Ali stopped breathing. His heart felt like it was going to burst, the room swam around him, and his gut could have been punched by a heavyweight prize fighter, right in the solar plexus. The physical reaction occurred long before he had mentally processed the obvious. The Colonel's name was Jack, not Jacques, and Sanders was an attempt to explain the word colonel, not the French word 'kernel'. He didn't integrate the information either then or later in a piecemeal fashion. He just knew, to the depth of his being, that the man recently hired by the Council to lead the university, the man who was his new boss, the man who was making waves with his tough enthusiasm to move the university forward as a great institution of learning, was the man who had tortured and killed his wife, his beloved Adilah. This was the man who had turned sweet beautiful Adilah into a broken, bloodied body, discarded on the street like a sack of garbage.

From that moment on Ali was consumed with only one thought: how to make Jack Michaels and the people who had appointed him suffer. There was no moral weighting of values or principles. He may not have been a Muslim, but he carried the ancestral archetype of justified revenge. There was no doubt in his mind as to the need to kill him. But how, exactly? He didn't want to just walk up to him and shoot the bastard. He himself would likely be killed or spend the rest of his days in prison. That would not avenge Adilah's suffering. Suicide by police was not on his agenda. All America was on edge. Police all over the country were brazenly shooting suspects dead. He wasn't like those poor pathetic Arab youths who had been tricked by religious zealots into believing suicide missions would insure their place in paradise surrounded by virgins. Ali had long ago concluded the Muslim faith was superstitious nonsense and a misogynistic, medieval religion that resembled the worst of Christianity five hundred years ago. His people hadn't moved with the times—Arabs were once the leading mathematicians and scientists in the ancient world, and now they were ignorant, hostile, brutal thugs knowing nothing but four generations of extreme sectarian violence ever since the old Ottoman Empire had been carved up by the European powers after World War I. Thanks T. E. Lawrence, but you failed. Ali wanted revenge, not martyrdom.

And then Curtis Pierson obligingly came into his office, a worthless human being only interested in getting drugs for himself. Here was a suitable decoy duck if ever there was one. Ali had already worked through and rejected several other scenarios when Curtis sauntered into his life. Here was a despicable person, vulgar, racist, and aggressive in Ali's view, who might prove to be a possible scapegoat, a distraction to the main event, someone who could be easily framed. Three remarkable openings presented themselves. First, he learned Curtis owned a Glock pistol. Second, that Curtis had discovered the chief of campus police was a member of some right-wing white power group, a fact that, if known, would result in Gary Finch's instant dismissal.

Third, it turned out the god Ali didn't believe in came to his aid. Curtis boasted that every Tuesday at about five o'clock he went to the library, no not to study, fuck that, but because the librarians allowed students to access the Keurig coffee machines free, and some sucker on the student council had suggested they put out free doughnuts at the same time. Curtis was the type of deviant personality who could be counted on to follow routines that were to his advantage—like free stuff. It was a popular event and there were lots of students milling about, so you had to get there right on five if you didn't want to be left with the second choice, sissy crème-filled doughnuts, Curtis had explained. Okay, good, perfect in fact, consistency was crucial.

When Ali went to Vermont for the weekend, he found it easy to buy the same model Glock pistol as Curtis had been boasting about. No questions asked at the gun show. He also entered an Internet café and opened an e-mail account. His user name he wanted to be 'Glock...something', but it was staggering how many versions had already been taken. Eventually he had to settle for a strange combination, wrote a corny, mildly threatening poem using Curtis's initials, and sent it to Katrina.

The trouble with Katrina was that she was a decent person and a caring, but inexperienced psychologist. Despite Ali feeding her some of his psychiatric impressions, Katrina had gone along with her supervisor and decided she could work with Curtis in a positive fashion, relying on interpersonal psychotherapy tactics. Fortunately, her old mentor Emeritus Professor Dave Gordon had disagreed, warning Katrina to look out for active threats or past incidents of violence. And that necessitated the last element of the deception—write a false 'confession', claim it came from Curtis, and fill it with sufficiently vague threats to fit Dave Gordon's criteria for dangerousness. Include sufficient specific detail to make it clear Curtis was planning mayhem on Tuesday at five in the library.

The only thing Ali had to do was find out Michaels' schedule on Tuesday afternoons. Allah, who doesn't even exist, be praised—on the first Tuesday of each month, Michaels has a Senior Leadership Team meeting then, along with members of the University Council, the very scum that had appointed the general in the first place. They'd get theirs. The meeting would stop at five for wine and cheese. All Ali had to do was walk in at about ten to five and let justice prevail—give Michaels five minutes of terror before systematically drilling his arms and legs. On the other side of campus, the wild, irresponsible shooting would start as Curtis sauntered unsuspectingly into view of the waiting police. The five-minute gap between incidents would be explained by Curtis being able to sprint across campus to the library after slaughtering the big shots in the Council boardroom. Curtis said he owned a Glock pistol. Ali now had the same model, with two extra magazine clips; no eyewitnesses could be left alive. The suspect would be blatantly obvious no one would bother to even try to match bullets.

It was still risky, full of holes, nice pun; lots could go wrong. But it was the best plan he'd been able to come up with after weeks of thinking of little else. Like Hamlet agonizing over revenge, Ali had thought through hundreds of possible scenarios. It consumed him and interfered with his work. It was hard being an effective psychiatrist when his own emotional state was deeply disordered. And there was the danger Michaels might connect him to Adilah's murder. Surely, in the course of their exchanges, she would have mentioned the name of her husband, working in a hospital in Sadr City? Wouldn't he have remembered such details? What if he found a way to silence Ali before he could confront him? Another of Hamlet's worries.

Elaborating these feelings of being in personal danger from this evil man intensified Ali's determination to bring him down. To strike first, to cut the head off the snake before it could coil up to make its lunge. The snake was pure evil. Killing it easily overrode the Hippocratic Oath.

Ali took pains to keep a low profile. He avoided any meetings in which Jack Michaels would be present or chairing or even organizing. He hoped the Arabic version of their names would be a source of confusion and thus disguise. Maybe Adilah would have used her maiden name, Sharine. That would make sense. Everything was so fraught and chaotic in the months leading up to Operation Iraqi Freedom, and then, as the bombs began to fall, humanity itself was suspended. Why had he agreed for her to work for the hated Ba'athist regime, even though the research she was conducting could potentially save lives and aid in the detection of terrorist activities involving explosives? They loved each other and had been happy together. Maybe, as Ali got more and more involved in his medical career, Adilah had started to feel a little neglected, a little left out. She was a modern Arab woman with an American college degree and acquired American sensibilities and values. Maybe she needed her own career to be validated, her demanding work to succeed. Maybe she wanted the respect that both his colleagues and his patients showed Ali, with his Yale M.D. and his charming style. The tiny element of guilt over her death took Ali over the edge.

Over the edge did not mean chaos. Mass killers are sometimes deliberate in their executions, sometimes wildly out of control. The final coming together of his plan so perfectly gave Ali an immense inner calm: cold, calculating, focused.

At precisely four forty-five he strode purposefully, but unhurriedly, just like the casualness of the 9/11 terrorists in Logan Airport, to the George Pataki Building, and up the stairs to the conference room. There was no one around; Michaels' excellent PA was not at her desk. She had been asked in to the meeting to take the minutes. Pity, Ali thought, that taking minutes would mean certain death. There was laughter from behind the door. Ali grabbed the impressive brass handle, and walked in.

Chapter 26: Second Thoughts

Roger and Curtis's progress through the drains was laboriously slow. Curtis had been injured when he fell down one of the tunnels and landed on his still painful ankle. Some of the drains were so narrow they both had to crawl along, and Roger was not physically up to it. He was nauseous—he was sure he was about to throw up or have a stroke. He had to stop and catch his breath and wipe the sweat from his face with his sleeve. This resulted in Curtis pushing his Glock pistol hard into Roger's butt, and saying:

"Get a fucking move on; we're running out of time. Don't you understand timing is everything? To frame me, Abidi has to do his thing a little before five."

Roger was far too terrified to process any of this. As he crawled along the tunnel, he grew increasingly panicked he'd made the biggest misjudgment of his life. It would go down as the dumbest example of gullibility in history. When he had unlocked the gate, and let out a potentially dangerous killer, he had been partially persuaded by the fantastical story. Sitting in the dark with a gun to his head, he had thought Curtis had made just a fraction of sense. Who could possibly spin a story like that? But in the bewildering time warp of seemingly endless tunnels, it began to dawn on him that Curtis could have long ago concocted some fantasy about Ali and ISIS, and might need to use it to get out of a sticky situation. It could have been rehearsed.

There was another element to the rash decision to let Curtis out of what was a very effective prison. For Roger, creeping and crawling through the drains, wild thoughts flooded over him, despite his terror. He had bought time by one daring action, but had he made matters any better? This was his moment, his life test, his ultimate trial. Back at the meeting of the security committee, he had faced his one and only test of leadership in his life and he had failed. He had confronted a challenge that maybe people like Jack Michaels as a military officer had faced many times before. Maybe even Gary Finch, whom he despised, had faced such challenges in his own line of security work. Real police officers faced it every day: how to choose between two highly risky moves when one lacked the essential information to make an informed split-second decision? You must go with your gut.

It was contrary to all of Roger's training as a scientist. Even unglamorous building scientists sometimes made life and death decisions about the safety of structures. If you were unsure, you gathered more data. It was his intellectual axiom. But there, in the committee room, in the excitement, he'd been swayed by emotion. He had listened to Katrina, not because she had the best possible information, but because he had discovered that she, as did he, liked to crack the hard sugar topping of a crème brûlée with the edge of the dessert spoon. And because of that they had laughed together, and because of that he had become infatuated. And because of that he had failed to challenge her on the adequacy of her evidence.

He could see why she thought what she thought, and why she was convinced. But it was his role as a leader to question the source of her certainty. What were her data? And it would have turned out her data was based on hearsay; the evidence came from a source that—whether Curtis was making everything up or not—had the potential to be unreliable, even fabricated for other ends.

Maybe it was Roger's fear that gave him a bizarre moment of insight. The US decision to invade Iraq had been difficult in a similar way. In the dilemma confronting George W. and Colin Powell, there were terrible costs for attacking Iraq and destroying Saddam Hussein, but there might have been terrible costs not to have done so. Roger and all his liberal friends were endlessly critical of the decision to invade Iraq, full of righteous indignation, just like the handful of left-wing senators who also voted against the move. But none of them had any reliable data either—their judgment was not inherently better than the President's. They were just fucking lucky their prejudice against warfare and intervention happened to be right on this occasion, just as Neville Chamberlain's attempt to appease Hitler happened to be wrong.

Quite possibly, in the Situation Room, some eager, intense, attractive, persuasive CIA officer had offered an opinion about Saddam Hussein that was not unlike Katrina's emotional opinion of Curtis Pierson—a dangerous psychopath, capable of anything. And that person was listened to, for God knows what unfounded reasons. The evidence was suspect, and everyone should have known it. The evidence here in the tiny inconsequential world of a security committee in little CVSU in little Fenton was also suspect. With suspect evidence, there should be caution—not hard, premature, for-or-against decisions.

Roger became even more distraught as he realized his deeply-held critique of the stupidity of the Bush decision on Iraq had just been demolished by his own analogous behavior. All he saw now was the glaring difficulty of committing to drastic action when inaction might have drastic consequences of its own. Were there no intermediate steps possible? That was the question he was faced with down there in the drain. What if a lower-key, less destructive but powerful military operation against Saddam had given the dictator the opportunity to stop boasting about weapons he didn't have? What if Chamberlain had tried compromise but from a much less naïve, much more hostile vantage point?

"What if?" questions defy answers and Roger knew it, but sometimes it's possible to step back from the cliff edge, isn't it? Were *two* atom bombs on civilian cities essential to convince Japan to surrender? Could just one active bomb and one dud labelled "Boom, the next one like this will wipe out this city," be considered pulling back from the brink? Roger's mind was racing—it was like he was having a manic episode, but it allowed him to realize he could still pull back from his brink.

As his wild thoughts exploded into consciousness, like a fireworks display in the night sky, he saw in the sudden illumination he didn't have to believe or not believe Curtis. If he took Curtis to the library and they found a spot with cell phone coverage, he could hand the entire operation over to the authorities. Well-armed police officers could take Curtis into custody at the identical moment they would rush to the Pataki Building to see if an ISIS terrorist who had been undercover as a psychiatrist for seven years was about to blow up the university's senior leadership team.

Roger had at least recognized Finch and his henchmen were itching for a violent showdown. Maybe George W. had some of those types in *his* Situation Room. And because of that recognition, Roger had come up with a redemption plan for himself that was not entirely shock and awe for Curtis. Why were they down in the tunnels and the drains in the first place? It had been to mitigate the risk—ironically, the risk to Curtis. Now it was only appropriate to continue to use the tunnels wisely. Curtis held the gun, but Roger held the knowledge of where they were and where they were going. That made the situation more equal.

Curtis couldn't go anywhere unless Roger led him there. It wasn't too late to change direction. Why lead Curtis to the admin building where there were no police and merely helpless senior members of the university? Maybe it'd been his plan all along, and the library shit had been designed to throw everyone off the scent. It was possible. But either way, there needed to be some means to even up the situation they were in. And leading Curtis to the library would allow him to be arrested if he was the shooter, and they could then, up on ground level, send emergency texts to warn the President and the Council people. Maybe they could lock and bar the door. He knew what he had to do. He crawled on.

Near the library exit from the drains, Roger stopped and begged Curtis for a rest. It was no ploy, but it was a big mistake. As they sat there with Roger breathing heavily, Curtis was looking around above them using his flashlight.

"There are markings on these drains that seem to identify what they are connected to. Back there I saw the letters MBL stenciled onto the wall. I figured that might be microbiology labs. It means these fucking awful tunnels are not quite as mysterious and incomprehensible as you like to pretend, old man. But now we must move on. Are the letters GPB somewhere here?"

Curtis waved his flashlight around some more and then came to dead stop. Above his head were the letters LTN.

"You idiot," he screamed. "That stands for Library Tower North. You cheating scumbag, you've led us to the fucking library after all."

He moved towards Roger as though he were going to throttle him there and then, but this time Roger was having none of it. He'd maneuvered Curtis this far, and right above them were four or five heavily armed police officers. The whole matter could be settled in a moment. He kicked out as hard as he could at Curtis, missed his head but struck him on his bad ankle. Curtis yelped in pain. Curtis raised his pistol and brought it down hard on Roger's head. He was angry. He had to stop him. He didn't care if he killed the fat shit.

Oh fuck, what had he done? He thought he had convinced the idiot, and now look. Roger slumped down on the ground. It was a powerful blow despite the narrow spaces. Roger was unconscious, out cold, but Curtis was lost. He had been following Roger in an overly trusting manner, and now he didn't know which direction anything was. He looked at his watch. Four forty-eight. The white knight riding in to the rescue to win fame and fortune was late and lost. Fuckin' hell. He stuffed his pistol into his belt, and, ignoring the pain in his ankle, he ran stooped, scrabbled, and crawled like a manic crab back to where he'd seen the microbiology lab sign. Triangulation—it was the only possible way in this dark underworld to estimate direction. Desperately trying to remember the layout of the campus buildings, he moved as fast as he was able along tunnels he could only guess were in the direction of the George Pataki Building, GPB.

Chapter 27: Execution

Ali entered the council room with its big conference table, and slammed the door behind him. Everyone turned to him and stared.

"I'm sorry, this is a private meeting. You've come to the wrong place, you have to leave." President Michaels was firm and cool.

Susan Kraus exclaimed in surprise: "It's Dr. Abidi. Is there something wrong, Ali? What can we do for you?"

Ali knew he had only a short advantage at the instant of surprise. He had to act fast. He pulled out the Glock pistol and pointed it around the room. Everyone could see it was a gun. There was a frozen moment.

"Put your cell phones on the table and push them towards the middle." He didn't realize it, but he was yelling. "If I see anyone touch their phone or try to get up, it will be the last thing you do on this earth." To emphasize it, he pressed the gun hard up against the neck of an older Council woman who had been sitting closest to the door. She and two others screamed.

"Shut up, and do as I say."

Ali walked fast up to the head of the table until he was standing close to Jack Michaels, who was surprisingly calm.

"Now look here man, put the gun down. Don't be a fool. We can sort this out—"

"Yes, we can," said Ali, and shot him in the leg.

Michaels doubled over in pain, holding his leg with both hands. "Jesus Christ, are you mad?" he shouted defiantly, and more people in the room were now shrieking or sobbing, or whimpering something. It looked like one of them might be getting up out of his seat and making a lunge towards Ali, so he swung his gun around and the man collapsed back in his seat. Ali now placed the pistol against Jack Michaels' head.

"Now is the time you'll feel what I feel: to know that you are dead, like I have been, or soon to be dead, in your case. Your crimes cannot even begin to be absolved, and my only joy is that I see fear deep in your eyes. Fear this, you piece of filth. This one is for Adilah, feel the pain."

Quickly moving the gun from Jack's head, Ali shot him in the other leg. This time Michaels screamed in agony.

"Is this how Adilah died, you animal? Is it? Do you feel it? You know I'm going to kill you slowly you butcher, you coward."

Michaels looked up, with a tortured expression, but through the pain it was an expression of total bewilderment. It was as though he was unable to comprehend what was happening, and he said nothing for a while. Two of the Council members were sobbing loudly, clinging to each other in terror.

"Adilah?" Michaels grunted.

"Yes, Adilah. Adilah Sharine."

"You've got it wrong. I loved Adilah."

Ali Abidi had thought he could not experience any more intense rage inside than he had been feeling since discovering Jack Michaels' true identity. There is surely some upper limit to hate, to rage, but apparently not. Instead of the dark blackness that had consumed him, there was, as he heard those three blasphemous words, an explosion of white hot fire in his body and mind. He aimed his gun at Jack Michaels' slumped torso and pumped four shots into him in rapid succession, screaming with each one and striking his own head with his other hand. He yanked Michaels' head backwards by his hair. His eyes were flickering but he was still conscious. The white heat extinguished and the cold blackness returned.

"Good," he snarled at him, "you sit there and enjoy dying. I've got nine more rounds in this clip, which looks like it will just be right to punish this group for choosing a piece of pig shit for their president, but they will die quicker."

Someone round the table screamed: "We're innocent!"

"As was Adilah, so I'll have mercy on you. I'll execute you first."

As Ali leveled the gun at her head, the door burst open. Ali had neglected to lock it. Curtis stood in the door. With little time to survey the scene, Curtis was quick, like a cat with a mouse. "Hey there doc, I'm back!"

Holding his right wrist with his left hand to steady his aim, Curtis squeezed off two rounds. Ali jerked backward. Curtis was a good shot, even from the other side of the room. Ali fell, motionless. Everyone screamed hysterically.

"For Christ sake, stop screaming. Call 911. Is Michaels still alive? He needs medical attention. Get your fuckin' phones."

In the moment of total silence before they complied, there was only the rasping sound of Jack Michael's feeble breaths. And then in the far distance a volley of what sounded like rifle fire, multiple shots rang out.

"What the fuck?" Curtis growled.

Chapter 28: Brain Drain

It was pitch dark when Roger MacDonald came to his senses. In the movies, people who have been knocked unconscious pick themselves up after a while and carry on as before. But it's not like that. Roger was disoriented and could barely sit up. He put one hand to his throbbing head and felt the blood trickling down his face. "Christ, I'm bleeding."

It took him a moment to remember where he was or what was happening. The pain in his head was unbearable, but he knew something had to be done. He reached in his pocket for his smartphone and turned on its flashlight. Had he failed? He moved the beam from left to right and looked around. Curtis was gone. He looked up at the hatch leading to the library. It was still closed. Thank God. Curtis had not killed students in the library, and he had not killed him.

Trying to focus his eyes on his phone, he saw the little radio signal he'd been waiting for so long. He had a 4G signal. He was back in range.

He staggered to his feet and reached in another pocket for the special wrench that opened the hatch. It was fine. It opened easily. He wanted to call someone, but that wasn't protocol, not the protocol his committee had worked on in crises. Use the special text number. What the shit was it? Double o seven? No, too predictable. #009. That's better. He typed in his text message, his fingers still trembling as he pressed the keys on his Android: "COMING IN NOW." **Send**.

It was the worst text message anyone ever wrote. If only he'd said, "*I'm* coming in." Or if only he had said 'coming up', since it was only he who was supposed to be down below the ground in the very drains which had made him famous. Or even possibly 'coming out'. But he did not send any of those messages, and the waiting posse knew only that Roger was close by, letting them know Curtis, the deranged killer, had been sighted approaching, and was coming into the library.

Roger opened the hatch and because there were some iron rungs in the form of a short ladder, he hauled himself up to the library basement level. His vision was blurry again and he felt faint. He staggered up the stairs to the storage room where he was supposed to be waiting, but no point waiting now, Curtis was gone. He opened the storage room door. In front of him were the swing doors into the library foyer.

Holding his hand up to his face and head to stop the bleeding, he thrust open one of the doors, and was met with a hail of bullets slamming him violently back against the door, his whole body twisting and writhing from the withering fire power as he crashed to the ground.

Chapter 29: Adilah

When the gunfire across campus subsided, the silence was suddenly split by the wail of ambulances, police cars and fire trucks.

"For Christ sake, get on your phones and tell them to hurry to get over here. The president is still alive but he's fading." Curtis was giving orders. The sheriff who rides in on his horse and saves the day gives the orders.

Two people helped Jack Michaels to the floor, his head on a rolled-up jacket, and ripped clothes and paper napkins were being pressed against the wounds in his abdomen and chest. Blood was trickling out of his mouth.

"Who's best with first aid?" Susan shouted. "We're losing him."

Jack's eyes flickered again, and he appeared finally to be losing all consciousness. It has often been said that when you are near death, your whole life flashes before you. How impossible to prove. And yet it is a fact that people often report everyday dreams as though they occurred over a long period of time—being lost, or searching for something. They seem to go on for hours, but the REM sleep records show they often last just a few minutes. For Jack, some of the most intense moments of his life returned, like a dream and just as vivid, against a background of light and sounds and the incoherent firings of failing neurons as the blood supply to his brain dissipated.

215

"Adilah, Adilah Sharine. That's my name." The young woman standing in front of him was slender and beautiful, with olive skin and classic Arabic features. She was dressed in an orange jumpsuit, prison garb, and yet she was elegant, graceful. Jack nodded and made a note in the file.

"Please sit down, Miss Sharine. Can I get you anything? A coffee? A glass of water?"

"What I would like is an explanation. What am I doing here? Am I under arrest? I've told you my name. What is yours?"

She spoke fluent English with a soft accent Jack couldn't place. A French lilt, perhaps, even an American sound—east coast? She was taller than Jack, and having her sit balanced things against her assurance and her stern questions. She was no ordinary person; alluring was the word that kept coming into Jack's mind. Could she be unaware of her own beauty, with her huge dark eyes and lips that could have been Botoxed, but undoubtedly weren't? Did she know her shy smile said, "Come here and kiss me"? No wonder Arab men covered their women if there were any others as gorgeous as she.

"My name is Colonel Jack Michaels. My apologies we had to bring you into this base. It is for your own protection; we call it protective custody, not arrest. I'm the commanding officer of this unit, and our job is to ensure there are no secret weapons programs still active, especially chemical weapons that might be deployed against your people, or ours. From your identification papers, I have ascertained you were trained in the States and have a degree in Biochemistry, and that you have been doing research in the explosives lab we have uncovered. Understand please this is strictly a security check, and as soon as possible, you will be free to go. You are also free to make a phone call if there is someone who will be worried about your safety."

Adilah looked at him. Like so many American men she had met in college, there was a natural charm, but you could not trust them because their social skills disguised their true feelings. A phone call would reassure her family, but it would also be monitored, for sure and she did not want to bring her mother, or worse still her husband Ali into it. *The less the Americans know the better*, she thought.

She shook her head. "I have no one," she lied.

"Okay, then, the sooner you tell me the truth about your work, the sooner we can get you out of here."

"Since I returned to Iraq from America, I've been employed in a research lab. It was funded by Saddam's cronies in the military, but it had attracted some of the top chemical engineers in the country—and elsewhere, some are from Egypt. The Ba'athists were so terrified of terrorism within their own country they were supporting research on the detection of explosives. That was what I was doing. I felt it acceptable because we were not manufacturing explosives but discovering ways to identify them. I'm a believer in peace. I figured it could save lives by reducing the effectiveness of terrorists, of whatever persuasion.

"We were making progress. We'd tried different methods. You Americans in your crime labs had gotten expert at detecting gunshot residue. But we soon discovered the swabs used by your TSA to detect glycerin are useless—lots of false positives from hand soap and stuff, which doesn't matter, but worse, far too many false negatives. Sniffer dogs are good, but the training takes forever, and the dogs run around randomly. In a mock-up baggage carousel in our lab, our best dog, led around by a handler, missed three percent of the positive items. It was because the handler was easily distracted by suspicious-looking fake passengers, or attractive ones, or new-looking suitcases. I was working on sensors that could detect molecules from the common explosives. These sensors could be used in standard x-ray devices, or on the roadside to detect passing cars which might have a car bomb. I felt we were doing something of value.

"I'm telling you everything I know, Colonel, but there is a lot I don't know. Somehow party officials heard about our progress and decided the lab had to be moved and the work had to be done in secret. The lab I was in, that your men discovered and where I was arrested—"

"Taken into protective custody."

"Splitting hairs doesn't make it feel any better, Colonel, but as I was saying, my lab remained where it was, but some of the best technicians and scientist were moved to a secret facility. It was rumored their job there was to discover explosive materials that could never be detected, or that could be enclosed in such a way no molecular traces would ever be released. I panicked; I'm very scared. Discoveries like that could make it far easier for terrorists to operate around the world. It would be much worse than those plastic handguns your country likes to manufacture."

Jack looked at her, thoughtfully. She was being open and honest, maybe too much so. He needed to stop lusting after her and switch to full interrogation mode—psychologically, not with coercion. Focusing, he asked her lots of questions about what she thought about the US operation in Iraq. She cried. She said it was horrible, that she had loved America when she was there and felt liberated, so she couldn't understand how they could justify the killing of so many innocent people, people she knew, family members. Without a doubt, she was glad Saddam Hussein was gone, good riddance, but what was going to fill the vacuum? Hoping to extend her US student visa, she had taken a civics class at night in New Haven. She knew about the Constitution. She asked Jack if the American leaders were so dumb that they thought some Iraqi Thomas Jefferson or Alexander Hamilton was going to pop up and create a democracy in a country which has been at war with itself since ancient Babylon, two thousand years before Mohammed? He shrugged and agreed they hadn't thought that far ahead. She was amazed to find that although he was probing her loyalties, he seemed genuinely to agree with everything she said. Maybe there was hope for the Americans yet.

A day later she was given back her clothes, along with some brand-new outfits exactly her size. Two days later, in Jack Michaels's office, they were drinking coffee and sharing candied citrus peels and fried almond pastries. When he asked her if her religion allowed her to drink wine, she laughed and said, "What religion might that be, Colonel? In New Haven, we drank California merlot; it was all we could afford."

Three days later, dressed in civilian clothes (Jack) and a Western dress (Adilah), they were eating filet steak and drinking Stag's Leap Cask 23 in a small private dining room somewhere on some base. They talked about their backgrounds, their interests, their hopes for the future—it was very much like a date and quite romantic. Adilah did not mention a husband.

They had been driven there in a Cadillac look-alike with a Chevrolet Kodiak diesel engine. "It's not quite as well equipped as the President's car, but it's a safe ride in this god-forsaken town," Jack had joked. On the ride back, slightly tipsy, Adilah wondered if this was the moment he would come on to her. But he did not. He was a perfect gentleman.

That night, thinking it all over, Adilah realized, with some shame, she would not have minded if he had come on to her. She had been away from Ali for so long, now he was working long hours in the central city, dealing with traumatized civilians and ex members of the Republican Guard. And Jack, unable to sleep, thought of nothing but her smile, her eyes, and the lovely almost French-like way she called him 'Jack' with an elongated vowel and a soft 'sha' sound rather than a harsh 'jah' sound.

Colonel Michaels had developed a plan, not of seduction, but of state security. He put it to Adilah hesitantly. "If we send you back to your lab with some well-crafted stories of rough interrogation, would you be willing to serve as an informer, trying to find the location of the new program?"

"A spy for you Americans?"

"Yes, you could put it like that."

"How else?"

"It would have to be top secret. To protect you, I wouldn't even tell my higher-ups about it. No CIA. I'd be your handler, me only. For your safety. We'd meet up occasionally, but all your reporting would be verbal, face-to-face. No phones, no e-mails, no disappearing ink. No briefcases left in the Baghdad bus station."

"Goodness, here I thought you were beginning to like me as a friend, and now I discover you were just trying to recruit me."

She was smiling, but Jack blushed. "Not beginning to. I do like you. I feel bad about asking you to do this, but I think it is the only way. You yourself admitted that technology to allow non-detectable explosive devices would be awful in the wrong hands."

"American hands are not the wrong hands, Jack?"

"Sometimes, but we try to be decent. We want peace in the Middle East. I wouldn't ask you to do this without some reward. If you get me the information, I'll get you back to anywhere you want to go. You said Iraq has no future for you and that you'd love to return to the States and do a doctorate and be a professor for peaceful technology. I could arrange it. Believe it or not, I'm hoping to get the hell out of this place and go into academia myself."

"Is that a proposition, Jack?" She gave one of her glorious, but gently mocking smiles. God, he adored this woman.

It was arranged. It took time for her to be accepted back in the facility. The management had not changed. There were potential enemies everywhere. She was careful and didn't ask too many questions. She had strictly private thoughts about what chemical elements of an explosive device made them least detectable. Maybe she could parlay some creative ideas to gain access to the other lab.

Then when she was due to make her third or fourth short report on her progress, meeting outside a mosque, a young Arab man with an American accent told her Jack had been injured. In a hasty conversation, he told her the name of the hospital. It was American, but if she said Colonel Michaels's name they would let her through. She was distressed to see his injuries. "They're just superficial," he claimed, "but my ankle is stuffed. When they let me out can you come and visit me? I've managed to get an apartment inside the green zone. Go to the US Embassy and they'll give you a secure pass."

She did. Why, she never completely understood, but she was lonely and scared. Being a spy for the Americans was traitorous and not popular. Jack was gentle and kind. When they kissed, he told her he loved her. She wasn't quite ready to say the same words, but she held him close, and she came with a passion and intensity she had never felt before. He was a good lover, despite the injured ankle—maybe because of it. He had to be careful, be tender, and take his time.

In the last remaining images of subconscious memories and feelings chiseled into his brain, the dying Jack Michaels saw her sweet face, felt her soft touch. There was light around her radiant body. "I love you, I adore you Adilah, why did you leave me?"

Adilah had suddenly disappeared. Secrets cannot be kept for long. Her pass to the US compound was discovered. She was exposed. Insurgents, another round of hate-filled violent men consumed by false Islamic faith, took her away and tortured her. They had managed to extract her mother's address. She said little else. As a message to the Americans, they left her, still alive, but only just, on the sidewalk outside their family villa.

What could Jack do? The operation had been a secret. Not until high level inquiries from the Army Medical Corps filtered through to his intelligence unit did he realize he had to answer his superiors' questions. Adilah's mother was talking. People were outraged. It looked like another savage American misuse of torture. The US Ambassador was asking questions. It had to be hushed up. Colonel Michaels had made a terrible error of judgment.

Why? Had he become romantically involved with someone he was illegally running as a spy, without any authority? "Look at these pictures, Colonel," they demanded. Jack vomited. Then they knew. "Because of your outstanding record and your injury, we'll cover it up," they assured him. "We will make plans for you to be transferred. Iraq dehumanizes the best of us. No one can take this situation for long."

Jack went to Hawaii. He was an excellent analyst of military strategy and policy. He was promoted, his record redacted. His commanding general agreed that resigning and pursuing his dreams of research and academia was a good career choice for him. Introducing distinguished military officers to those awful, closed, hypocritical, left-wing campus communities would be excellent. But not a day passed that he didn't think longingly of Adilah, even when he met and fell for Tomoko, and they got married and went to Nashville for his doctorate. They made a good life together. She enjoyed the academic prestige. But when Susan Kraus tried gently to tell her of Jack's last breaths and words on the floor of the council chamber, Tomoko didn't want to hear them. She didn't want to know.

Chapter 30: The Final Chapter

"Hi Curtis, come on in, real good to see you," Katrina was grinning broadly.

"I've come to say goodbye, Katrina. Hey, do you think we can go outside somewhere to talk? The clinic gives me a bad vibe, and sitting here with you is too much of the doctor-patient relationship. There's a bench in the Stickley Courtyard I like, which gets the afternoon sun."

He was a changed man. His tone was different, his affect new, softer.

"Who are you, and what have you done with my client?" Katrina joked, shaking her head.

When they had settled, Katrina gave Curtis a quick update: "Susan Kraus, the provost, is now Acting President. I'm sure the Council will give her the permanent appointment. Gary Finch has been arrested and charged with manslaughter. Two of the other campus police officers have been dismissed and the rest suspended—with pay until the inquiry is finished, but I think they're all toast, except for the woman officer who was in the hospital having her appendix removed at the time.

"The Fenton police department has taken over campus security and all guns, even handguns, are locked up in their cruisers. Tomoko Michaels has left and gone back to the Big Island in Hawaii, where she has family. She's quite shattered, poor thing. The clinic's making a referral for grief counseling for her. The Senior Leadership Team is planning a big memorial service for Professor Roger MacDonald. The Faculty Senate passed a motion to rename the Building Science complex after him.

"As Susan Kraus told his sons when they got here, there were so many high-velocity bullets he'd never have known what hit him. He would have died instantly and without pain and without fear. Everyone agrees he was a hero. Small comfort. I've inherited his lovely cat, Eugène, although I'm not home enough to look after him properly. Good thing he's neutered. The reporters have finally gone and as you know there is going to be a special ceremony in the concert hall to honor you."

"I won't be going, Katrina. I'm quitting school. I'm leaving Fenton today. That's why I'm here: to say goodbye…"

"But, why?"

"I've got two good reasons. The first is that I'm going to Pennsylvania to try to make things right. I've hired a lawyer and we're petitioning the Governor for my birth mother's release from prison. She was innocent, just covering for my violence. We think we have a good case, now that I'm famous."

"So she didn't hang herself? Why did you lie about that?"

"I lied about most things. I guess I wanted you to feel sorry for me. And to deal with her complete removal from my life, I used to fantasize she was dead. Maybe I even wished it. The second reason is that I've got to get away from here…"

He stopped. Katrina's eyes were welling up with tears.

"Oh Curtis, I am so sorry. I feel so guilty. I totally misjudged you. I misled our security committee. I was terribly wrong and had such bad judgment…"

"No, you didn't. I'm a genuine nut case. You misled them only while thinking you were doing the right thing. It was Abidi who misled you all, knowingly and deliberately and with homicidal intent. You can't blame yourself. You know you had to breach confidentiality—it's in your ethics. You couldn't have done anything different."

"Oh my God, now who's the therapist here? You've no idea how that makes me feel."

Katrina was crying now and Curtis put his arm around her. She didn't pull away. She snuggled up closer to him and he smelled her hair and felt the side of her breast against his chest. But it gave him a feeling of deep peace and satisfaction. If he had not been so guilt ridden, all his bravado, his gun-toting hostility would have been unnecessary. His violent past had perverted him. Yet she had taught him, slowly and sensibly, to be able to feel simple affection again. She had, in her own therapeutic way, accepted him, worked with him despite her obvious dislike. He had behaved like a total prick. He still felt deep discomfort he had abused her privacy so badly. Her breach of his right to privacy was professionally justified and proper; his violation of hers was unacceptable. If only she had been able to see his hostility was a defense and that he liked her, admired her, valued her intelligence and her composure. She hadn't misjudged him: he was a danger, but not the stereotypical killer of her textbooks and journal articles.

After a long while Katrina sniffed, wiped her eyes, and asked him what he was planning on doing next.

"I'm not sure. Sorting out my mother is my first priority, but it scares me. How do we re-connect after all this time? And taking care of my mom here in Fenton is important. I've been offered a financial payout from the university and I'm giving most of it to my mom so she can quit working at the bowling alley. I'll keep a little to let me travel, go to places like Thailand, or Australia, places where you can walkabout. Reinvent myself. Give my mother a chance to adjust. Maybe you should be her therapist. She's going to have to move somewhere. You could give her BD's cat. You were always right about one thing Katrina, I'm a mess; I'm emotionally scarred. I've now killed two people.

"I don't think I ever told you this, but my birth mother was an Arab immigrant. She's from Jordan. Her English isn't real good—a second reason everyone thought her capable of killing her abusive husband.

"My father wasn't always like that, although as far back as I can remember I knew he had a vicious temper, often flying into a rage. By the time I was three, I had learned that if there were signs he'd been drinking I had to keep very quiet. My mother protected me and that made him aggressive towards her. I believe she had reported him to social services and he changed for a short while. You know about these things.

"My mother was in a weak situation. She was a Christian, although the neighbors and everyone around just assumed she was a Muslim. She often wore a headscarf. As do a lot of Catholics, but once you're typecast…well, shit happens. She was a refugee. She fled Jordan. Despite it being one of the safest countries in the Middle East, the Christian communities are discriminated against. I think my father was looking for an easy-going, dutiful wife who could be bullied. She wasn't. There was a lot of fighting.

"She told me stories about life in the Middle East, about Arab history and culture, and magical children's stories. Why do you think I was so interested in what was happening to Islamic refugees in the Southern Tier, and why I went to those screwed up meetings? I needed to know more about the plight of Arabs, which of course has gotten worse and worse. Everyone hates them and after I was taken away and adopted, I made sure no-one knew I was half Arab. I have dark skin. I said I had some Spanish grandparents and my name in Spanish would be Cortez. Shit, just further evidence of my fucked-up identity crisis. I couldn't work out most of these issues because I was mad and hostile all the time. I used my brains not to self-analyze but to sneer at the world."

He paused, reflectively. Katrina has never before seen him be insightful. Slowly, he said:

"It's a funny thing about the world and about fate, but it was going to those hate-group meetings and seeing stupid, diffuse, unfocused anger in those pathetic rednecks convinced me *I* needed therapy. I didn't want to end up like them. That's how I came to you."

Katrina raised her head off his shoulder, feeling a little awkward at being reminded he was her patient.

"It was your wild story about those meetings, Curtis, which finally convinced me you had a dangerous personality disorder, unable to separate reality from fiction. I've lived in this community for five years and I couldn't believe we had people like that."

"Well, there was some fiction! Any good story needs embellishment. But you live in a privileged ivory tower; you can't always comprehend the resentment, even mine." Curtis thought for an instant, and decided this was not the time for a full confession that would destroy this moment. Maybe one day.

"Let's just say I am still seriously fuckin' disturbed, and I can't any longer even pretend to be tough and important and better than other people—that was all an act to mask my self-revulsion: my shame at allowing my mother to be punished for my sins. I'm going to need more therapy. Lots of it. I'm damaged. But for now, I need a change. I need to change. It will take time. You say you feel guilty, however I owe you so much, more than you know, but the other big reason to get away is that I have to get away from you…"

Katrina looked up again, startled; her expression turned to puzzlement. He gazed intently at her.

"Because I love you, Katrina."

"But," Katrina began, and Curtis put his finger to her lips.

"Don't say a word. Don't say it cannot be, don't say you are too old, don't say I don't know you or anything about you, don't say it is common for patients to fall for their therapists, don't say it's unethical, don't say you have no reciprocal feelings for me—don't spoil the fairy-tale of my confession. Don't break the delusion. I know all those things to be true and I don't expect anything and I don't want any false words from you to try to make me feel better."

He stood up. He was leaving. Katrina moved towards him, put her arms around him, kissed him on the cheek and hugged him tight. He was trembling. He clung to her.

"I love you so much, Kat. I'll never forget you."

She kissed him again. Hesitated. What words safely described her feeling at that moment?

"I'll never forget you either, Curtis, as long as I live."
They knew they were both speaking the truth.

*****